Finding Abby

*For the little girl in the
brown wool dress*

Finding Abby

Virginia M. Scott

Butte Publications, Inc.
Hillsboro, Oregon

FINDING ABBY

© 2000 Virginia M. Scott

Editor: Ellen Todras
Cover Illustration: Brad Henson
Page Design: Anita Jones

Butte Publications, Inc.
P. O. Box 1328
Hillsboro, OR 97123-1328
U.S.A.

Scott, Virginia M., 1945-
    Finding Abby / by Virginia M. Scott. -- 1st ed.
    p. cm.
    LCCN: 99-67690
    ISBN: 1-884362-35-4

    1. Hearing impaired--Fiction.
    2. Self-perception--Fiction.   I. Title.

PS3569.C6793F56 2000   813'.54
                        QBI99-1466

─Acknowledgments─

For his professional expertise in the field of the education of the deaf, most notably his dedication to training teachers of the deaf and hard of hearing, as well as for his personal support, I would like to thank Dr. H. William Brelje, whose suggestions were invaluable in the writing of this book. Deep gratitude goes to my late mother-in-law, who introduced me to the world of the prelingually deaf and showed me that love transcends different communication modes; and to Matthew Snyder, whose unconditional love bridges gaps most magically. Special thanks to Mr. Linnemann, who, I hope, resides in a book-lined paradise. Last but not least, although this book is fiction, I could never forget the love of my parents, who faced my new condition of deafness along with me.

"Having been is also a kind of being, and perhaps the surest kind."

Viktor Frankl

‒PROLOGUE ‒

Abby *Chip, chip, chip* went the thundering sound of myself breaking into pieces that threatened to fly off into some awful void of nothingness under the chisels of people who included doctors, teachers, and even my parents. I could never fathom why, when they were trying to help me, no one seemed to want to get in touch with how I felt deep down inside. Why were they so focused upon my hearing that the real, essential Abby had become invisible to them?

The campaign to save my hearing included electrical stimulation, vitamin therapy, hormones, and testing every part of my body. It's good to have a healthy heart and sound liver, and I guess one needs to be poked and prodded and measured in many ways to find out what is working and what is not. I had scans, blood work and, of course, every hearing test known to humankind, but nobody ever asked how I felt about it or what my fears and hopes and dreams were.

It was as if getting some sound—any sound—into my one remaining ear made everything rosy, as if they were trying to take all those little pieces of me and reform them into this beautiful set of ears without a soul. We all agreed that I needed to communicate. What they didn't get was that my soul didn't clamor for sound. It cried for understanding and acceptance, and it needed the memory of quality sound, rather than the reality of unpleasant, unwanted noise, to feel nourished. But, oh, no, a little sound was better than none.

What was I, anyway? One more cookie out of a package? Were all people who didn't hear right chocolate mint? "Deaf people traditionally do well at math. You can excel here, too," a teacher had insisted in a futile attempt to turn me into something I wasn't. Who I was was Abby Jensen, math klutz extraordinaire, and some math angel hadn't suddenly touched me with aptitude as I lay in a coma. I had liked learning new words, reading, and writing before, and I still did, no matter what "tradition" said, and no matter what seemed "logical" for a deaf person to pursue.

I was still so normal, still so *me*, but they didn't see it. Take Jay Cassidy, for instance. I would be walking up the stairs between periods at school, and there he would be, coming down. I would see his slim form, chestnut hair, and those dreamy hazel eyes fringed with the lushest lashes imaginable, and my heart would go *ta-thunk, ta-thunk, ta-thunk* in a rhythm that threatened to explode right out of my chest. Did he see me, too? Did he even say something sometimes that I missed? Concentrating as I needed to on the stairs, especially with knees gone rubbery at the sight of him, I was never sure, and I died a little each time in not knowing.

What got me was how a "hi" from Jay Cassidy could matter so much to me, while those making important decisions in my life never even seemed to consider that I might have feelings for a guy and lots of other things that went beyond decibel levels, test scores, and their ways of charting my life. Who said I shouldn't play the piano anymore? Why would I automatically be effective at this or that when I hadn't been before? Who decided that it was okay for my social life to go to pot while I traveled to see still another doctor or took a drug that made me too sick to keep up with homework? It was like, *Aargh! Hear me, hear me, hear me!*

They didn't, though. Worse, as I started losing myself, I was terrified that all the broken bits of me would hurtle into the black hole of a reality that wasn't mine.

～Chapter One～

Opening the door to Abby's room had always been a little like walking through a gate and coming upon an unexpected, old-fashioned garden of cabbage roses, delphiniums, and other blooms strewn across her fluffy duvet and sprinkled haphazardly over the celadon, lattice-patterned rug. Abby wasn't English, but you'd never have known it from looking at the tea-stained pillow shams, the collection of small porcelain teapots on the shelf over her bed, and the artistic tablescapes she had created with a teacup here, an antique book there, and fresh flowers, even if they were just Queen Anne's lace plucked from the side of the road, in our great-grandmother's dented, silver creamer. She had a talent for putting things together in a most romantic way.

The tranquil setting was just so . . . Abby . . . that I struggled for my next breath. I closed my eyes and thought back to— was it just two days ago? That awful day in May, I had planned to tell Kent that it wasn't going to work out between us and that I wouldn't be taking the summer job in Chicago, after all. Little bursts of rehearsed speech had crept into my thoughts all week, so much so that I almost welcomed the crunch finals week demanded. The last, the toughest, was just over, and we had eaten out to celebrate my survival.

Back at my apartment after a dinner laced with the kind of fast-paced, stimulating conversation I appreciated as one of Kent's best qualities, I dreaded it even more. He made it worse as he unlocked the door and we entered. When he spoke, it was a compliment, and Kent through and through. "Do you know what one of the things I love the most about you is? Other than your sterling personality and honey-haired beauty, that is."

He winked.

"No, what?"

"The way you've turned this little place into a cozy

home."

"Molly deserves half the credit."

"I know, but what I see when I look around is you: the pictures of your family, the pillows I know you stitched by hand, and the African violets on the sill."

My hands were clammy. Why did he have to be such a nice guy? Still, it was because he was so decent that he deserved to hear the truth. "Kent, why don't you sit down."

"Oh, your machine is blinking."

"It's probably nothing. I'll get it later."

He shook his head and laughed, crinkling his face familiarly. "That's not the Paige Jensen I know."

I did have a thing about checking my machine. I smiled. "All right, all right. There's some iced tea in the fridge while you're waiting."

"I'll pass, but thanks."

It was probably just as well. One message wouldn't take long, and then I would finally get to my task.

Instead, everything froze as Dad's voice instantly mesmerized me. "It's 5:30 on Thursday. Come home as soon as you can, Paige. Abby's had an accident. We'll fill you in when you arrive."

An accident . . . .

In her room, I felt my fingernails dig into my palm. I picked up a shell gleaned from our trip to Sanibel Island, and as I held it to my ear, I thought I heard the ocean roar. For a moment, I saw a five-year-old Abby, pipestem legs pumping toward me because she had seen a crab.

"Paithe, it'th after me!"

I draped the new Minnie Mouse beach towel around her narrow shoulders and hugged her to me. Then I pointed to the crab, which by that time was joining another. "No, silly. It has a friend over there. Don't you see?"

Abby's April sky eyes grew as round as plates as they followed the distinctive movement of the crustaceans. She looked at me skeptically. "Uh huh, but I don't want to dream about crabth pinthing my toeth."

That had led to the purchase of Emma, Abby's toy flamingo, to stave off any nightmares about crabs.

The shell was still to my ear, but there was no sound of waves now, and when I looked around the room and spied Emma on the wicker rocker, I set the shell down and walked over to the plush toy that had become my sister's security blanket and sometimes, I suspected, her confidante.

About to reach for the long-necked, garish bird, I didn't, suddenly angry at the inanimate object for not having been able to banish whatever fears, whatever emotions, Abby had felt at the end.

My thoughts glazed over. The trip home to Oregon had been unreal.

"Abby . . . died, Paige," Dad, too choked up to say any more than that just then, had said with quiet finality at the airport. The words cut into me like rapiers, shredding all that was normal.

Dead meant withered roses, a pet turtle not there anymore, or a grandparent passing away. But this was my baby sister, and the word just didn't translate.

"Dead?"

Dad only nodded. His heartbreak was so real, so evident in his dull eyes, pasty face, and sagging form, that as stunned as I was myself, my instinct was to comfort him. It was when I put my arms around him and heard him moan that my heart also broke.

It was real. Abby was dead. The terrible knowledge unleashed a torrent of feelings and tears.

Finally, I asked, "Tell me what happened?" Images of car crashes, freak accidents, and sudden illness flitted through my thoughts, each one more horrible than the last, but when Dad spoke haltingly, the answer was worse than anything I had imagined.

"It was . . . suicide."

Suicide. Suicide? I shook my head. It had to have been a mistake. I knew my sixteen-year-old sister had abhorred the idea of taking one's own life.

In Abby's room, Emma's eyes stared back at me. What stories could she tell? What anguish? Then I looked again and saw them for what they were: plastic, only black plastic. The real question wasn't where Emma had been.

What about me? Where was I? During what turned out to be the last of my sister's life, I had been close to two thousand miles away, off at college learning things, having fun, and yes, I had to admit, getting away from Abby.

It wasn't that I lacked compassion for what she had gone through in getting sick, losing her hearing, and having her life turned upside-down, but it had also changed mine and the dynamics of our family life. Although in a way I understood it, it was still uncomfortable when my parents all but stopped being my parents and my sister alternated between being a very young child again and someone so old and sage that it scared me. The initial focus upon the sick Abby just never abated, so that our lives became a whirl of Abby's doctors' appointments, crushed expectations, flickering hopes, and plans gone awry. My needs, my accomplishments—my very role in the family—fell entirely by the wayside as my parents, often bickering, struggled to cope with the change in their younger daughter. I felt for them and for Abby, but I had learned how powerless I was to make things right again. Lonely in my own home, I wanted to be at a college far from turmoil that excluded me, and the transfer had freed me, leading me away.

Consumed now with guilt and regret, I sat on the edge of her bed. *Abby, oh, Abby, what if I had been here! Would you have opened up to me? Would I have heard your cry?*

I knew I would have at one time. Since we were born six years apart, we had never been "best friends" the way some sisters closer together in age are, sharing clothes and things, but we had a very special bond, nonetheless. Through her, I discovered the first stirrings of maternalism, just as in me, I think she found a spare mother. It wasn't that our mother fell short in being there for her, but it was just so often to me whom Abby ran with her skinned knees needing to be bandaged and me she emulated in sometimes irritating, other times humorous, or even flattering, ways.

I could remember the very first time I had held my baby sister and explored her tiny body in wonder at the pearl-sized toes and rosebud mouth. Even though I was still a child myself, I reveled almost as much as my parents did in Abby's first smile, her first words, and her first everything. As I had gone about the business of learning to print my name and running through the sprinkler with my best friend, Abby had developed from that helpless little wonder into a full-fledged person. When she became something of a music prodigy, I burst with pride.

Almost from the beginning, she was a little girl who seemed from another time. There was something ethereal about her very appearance, especially in the hair that rippled below her shoulders like a moon river, shimmering with pale blondeness that was somewhere between gold and silver. Her interests also hinted of an earlier time. She preferred a shiny red balloon to a sophisticated toy, classical to contemporary music, and books to cartoons and computer games. Even as a preschooler, she'd had a special sensitivity and appreciation of nature: "I want to reach right out and tickle those mountains." She led me to see things in new, sometimes better ways.

Reading to her became one of our special things when she was still very small. At four, she loved *A Child's Garden of Verses* and listened in rapt attention as I read, and reread, her favorite poem, "The Swing."

A lump came into my throat at the memory.

"Thing it to me, Paithe," she said in the lisp she carried with her until around the time she began school. So, I thought up a tune and sang the words as I pushed her higher and higher in our backyard. We had no garden wall, but since one figured prominently in the poem, Abby, being Abby, invented one, describing its stones and the imaginary hollyhocks in such detail that I also started seeing her vision. Inspired by the poem's wording, for years this or that was "the pleasantest thing" to Abby.

"Pleasant" to even a very young Abby was making people happy and helping others. She made May baskets, for example, filling construction paper cones with daffodils, tulips, and sprigs of flowering shrubs, to leave as anonymous surprises on people's doorknobs. She had a knack for knowing which neighbor was lonely and in need of a little cheer. Abby rang that person's bell and hid, watching as the recipient found her basket. "I'm celebrating spring," she told me, "and the best part is the smile on someone's face when she finds my present. It is just 'the pleasantest thing.'"

I looked out the window and saw the bright green Maytime grass, the candy pink of a rhododendron, and, in the foreground, the tender leaves of an alder that just missed brushing the upper story of our house. The swing was long gone, but for a moment, as if a photographic slide had dropped into my brain, I saw Abby's garden wall before the image drifted away as gently and as surely as an Oregon morning mist.

Perhaps trying to reclaim the vision, suddenly I had to know every word of the poem again. When I turned around and began looking for the Robert Louis Stevenson classic, though, I couldn't find it in plain sight. I sighed. I wasn't ready to peek into Abby's drawers and closet.

In one of the tablescapes, I did spot "Mouse Manual," however, its 2" x 2" size almost hidden by the stack of old children's readers that had belonged to our grandmother. "Don't ever throw it away," I had said of the manual. "It's so cute." And Abby had promised not to. Now, looking at its fake-leather cover, it was almost more than I could bear to see the little book, and yet its existence was, somehow, comforting.

Abby was a child of many talents. Her music had eclipsed most of them, but perhaps inspired by images in the old books she treasured, she had begun writing herself when she could barely string letters into words. Her first concerted endeavor was the minuscule directive to a bevy of imaginary, clothed mice on such topics as how to bell the cat. "Well, what would you do if you were a mouse and needed to know things?" she had asked, and it made all the sense in the world. As I looked at that effort now, I didn't have to open it to remember the crooked printing or the way I had helped bind the tiny "tome" with a darning needle and heavy thread.

Abby had continued writing. A new toy meant a story about it: dolls often were princesses from mythical kingdoms, and a balloon had, in Abby's way of thinking, floated to her from another little girl in a faraway land.

By the time she was eleven or so, she was writing a series of mystery stories called "The Mysteries of Alison and Abigail," with titles like "Tower of Fear," all featuring herself and her best friend, Alison Wang, as plucky junior sleuths. Some of her villains were obvious, with "eyes the color of swamp water," but Abby had such a way with words, and the heroines were so amusing, that it was easy to get caught up in the action of her fast-moving plots. I hoped the little stories would turn up somewhere.

Little stories . . . little stories? Something lurched in my chest as the memories of the young, carefree Abby frittered away, slipping effortlessly and inexorably into images of an Abby struggling with illness, hearing loss, and whatever demons had gone with them. Memories and little stories were all that was left, and I felt my heart break into a thousand pieces at the loss. My baby sister was dead.

Recollections of her post-illness life cut into me like shards of glass. Abby wasn't one to moon around and complain, but she looked so like a hurt rabbit, helpless and vulnerable, in her bed. I could see the unasked "Why me?" Why hadn't I sat down beside her and addressed that question? Oh, I knew. I knew the answer to that one. I'd wondered why, too, and I, like Abby, had no answer. Had my parents? Had anyone?

It wasn't that her life became totally bleak afterwards, but the changes were staggering. In the space of the week she was in the coma, she went from being an accomplished pianist who sometimes had prepared British high teas, complete with watercress sandwiches, for neighbors, and from a fourteen-year-old girl with secrets to whisper to friends, to someone suddenly cut off from music, from automatically helping others, and from easy-flowing socializing. It was almost as if when I looked into the blue eyes that had once held so much laughter and enthusiasm for life, there was a daze, a deadness.

"Paige?" The voice cut into my thoughts, and I jumped. Dad stood in the doorway, obviously unsure about coming in. "I didn't know you were in here."

I nodded. "Mom wanted me to—"

"Are you all right?" My voice had cracked, and whatever qualms he had had about walking into Abby's room were gone as he strode to the bed, sat down beside me, and held me as I cried. *No, no, no, Daddy. It's not all right. Make it go away.* The unspoken words merely spilled out as tears.

"I'm better now," I finally said, although "better" was certainly a relative term. I felt as though I were in the midst of a nightmare. "I came to find something for Abby to wear to the . . . funeral. How's Mom?"

"Out of it. Dr. Bader gave her a sedative. Are you up to finding a dress?"

I didn't want to be down on Mom during what had to be the most terrible ordeal of her life, but at the same time, I longed for her arms around me, her concern about her older daughter's seeking a burial dress for her little sister—just a mother's love. I was grateful at that moment for Dad's, and that current of love somehow gave me strength I thought I didn't have.

"Yeah, I'm okay with it. Someone has to."

It was after Dad left the room that Abby's pre-illness voice, all shot through with wonder, came to me: *Look, look at the stars, like thousands of lighthouses showing the way.*

When I eventually got up the courage to open the closet door, I unhesitatingly chose the navy blue dress with the big white collar adorned by a spattering of stars.

— CHAPTER TWO —

Abby Like a cloud shadow—random, floating, constantly changing tenor—was the loss of hearing in my life, with the power to transform any given moment from sunny to dark. What I noticed first were the holes where words, comprehension, and connections with other people had been. I heard, but in bits and pieces, and in struggling to put them together like some horribly complex jigsaw puzzle that would never get done, I felt limp from the effort, ineffectual, and deprived, for if I understood fairly well on one day, I might not the next; I might even end up with a day when almost every sentence came through like:"_____ . . . mumble . . . gargle . . . muted hissing," Paige said. *That* was English?

Sometimes I pretended to hear because I was embarrassed to admit that I didn't, or I was tired from trying to drink in intelligible sound, but this was my sister, who, of all people, had been patient.

"What?" I asked matter-of-factly, but there it was: the despised, too-often-used word that called attention to myself and sometimes raised hackles of irritation in others.

"_____ impatient _____," she repeated. Somehow, I got that one word, but not the rest of the sentence, and I felt my heart sink to my toes.

Oh, great! She was impatient with me now. What if my "What's?" started driving everybody away? The cloud shadow drifted over me, and I turned away, struck by a new kind of fear that was, if possible, already old and stale.

"*Aay,*" I heard. My sister was tapping my arm to get my attention, and I realized that the meaningless grating must have been Paige's customary "Hey," so I looked at her. She didn't seem impatient, but lots of people walked on eggshells around me, and she could be masking it.

"Hey what?"

She just looked at me. Then she reached for a pad of paper and scribbled: I THINK YOU MISUNDERSTOOD ME. WHAT DID YOU THINK I SAID? I KNOW THAT LOOK, ABBY.

"You're impatient with me," I said.

She gave me a weird look and then actually laughed, although it didn't seem to be at me. She wrote: I SAID I WAS GOING OUTSIDE TO WATER THE *IMPATIENS*.

I chuckled at my mistake. Little flowers: she had been talking about pink and white flowers, not her feelings for me.

The laughter never stuck with me for long, though. Holes, bits and pieces . . . . Where listening had once been so easy and spontaneous, it now took on the proportions of an Olympic event just to get small talk. My exasperation level varied from day to day, and from person to person, and sometimes got the best of me. I raged, I seethed, for what had been so simple, and still was to everybody else I knew.

"'I feel like poking my ears with an ice pick," I commented on another, better hearing day. Oddly, sometimes those days were harder on me than the bad ones, because on the better days, I was so close to the old, hearing me that I could almost taste the way it used to be. That I couldn't make it all the way back raised my frustration level to the nth degree.

"You don't really mean that," Paige said.

"Don't I?" Her expression clued me in to her frame of mind. "Oh, now don't go tell Mom. She'd freak."

"You won't really do something like that, will you? You _____."

Paige, who almost always remembered to face me when she spoke, forgot my new need and looked out the window. Even though it was a better hearing day than some, her voice trailed into nothingness, lost within the space of my room. Where did sound go, anyway, when it wasn't heard? Into the flowers of the drapes? Into the carpet? Nowhere?

She turned back around. "Abby?"

"No, of course not. I know I would just puncture my

eardrums. It's just . . . oh, I don't know."

"Just what?"

"I don't know if you can understand."

"Well, let me at least try."

"It's this, oh, burning urge to do something to pop whatever barrier it is so that I can hear right again. I can't stand this!"

In fact, not hearing right was so claustrophobic that I screamed when nobody was home, sure I would pierce that muffler in my ears and let all sound flood back in normally. I also tried shaking my head vigorously as one does after swimming. Maybe I could rattle my hearing back to normal.

Nothing worked.

Diminished hearing was only the prominent tip of a very large iceberg that formed so insidiously that I hardly saw it happening until I started ramming into it on an almost daily basis in increasingly destructive ways.

It all started with meningitis. For a long time, medically speaking, I was a mess. First, there was the illness itself. I had some of the symptoms, like the telltale crushing headache, and not others, such as the high fever, so nobody automatically assumed that it was anything major.

It was summertime, and my best friend, Alison, and I were at the food court in Washington Square. It had been such an ordinary afternoon of going from one store to another as we checked out half-price shorts and clothes for fall. We decided we liked the new colors, and of course we projected ahead to going back to school in almost nonstop conversation.

Sick? I didn't feel sick at all.

Then while we devoured our food, head and neck pain moved in as quietly and inexorably as a coastal fog. Suddenly very tired, I sighed and kept eating my three-cheese pizza and talking with Alison about topics as varied as music, boys, and the way there were so many different kinds of people in the mall.

"What language do you think they are speaking?" I wondered, focusing away from my discomfort as I referred to the trio at the next table. The cadence was very different from English, and I made out no familiar words, as I could with the Spanish that was becoming increasingly common in the Portland area. I had no inkling that I would never again be able to differentiate anything like that in such a noisy setting.

"Some Indian or Pakistani dialect," Alison guessed.

The lights in the food court seared my eyes without warning as fingers of pain pushed behind them and grabbed like a giant's hand at my very brain; my aching neck felt no stronger than a wobbly stem. I didn't realize I was sitting there with my hand supporting my head until Alison asked, "Are you all right, Abby?"

I started to tell her that it was just a little headache. I even considered taking an aspirin, but some strange instinct that it wasn't anything usual made me say, "No. I suddenly feel terrible. Let's call it a day."

At home, the headache only kept getting more intense, if possible, but since those other hallmarks of meningitis were absent, although they gave me a painkiller and soothed me, my parents didn't rush me to the hospital. Even my doctor father didn't see it for what it was. We'll never know if it was the delay in getting me there, and the way that gave the illness time to progress and ravage things, or the drugs they finally gave me to save my life that left me severely deafened. Something did, though, and maybe it doesn't matter what at this point.

I had just turned fourteen, and although I felt secure in my parents' love, it hadn't been the best couple of years of my life. I mean, who was I, anyway? A lot of the time, I felt like some kind of half-breed, caught between the little girl I had always been and the woman I was becoming, but wasn't quite. Take Emma, for example. Although I wouldn't have been caught dead in front of people with my stuffed toy flamingo from our trip to Florida when I was five, I sometimes curled up with her when nobody was looking. I didn't like being treated like a child, yet I felt a new kind of loss because part of me—the part that noticed how interesting boys were—signaled that it was time to think about putting Emma away.

Even something in my friendships was changing. Alison and I had switched from dolls, and then arts and crafts, to talking a lot about hair and clothes, boys, and futures that included big white weddings and careers more relevant to the social scene than being the glamorous, pink-sequined trapeze artists we had once made a pact to be. It was a time of letting go, which made it scary because we weren't sure what was out there to latch onto comfortably.

Still, if finding a comfort zone as a teenager was daunting, what was to come defies description.

Since I was in a coma at first, I don't remember much about having been in the hospital, but from the time I woke up, drifting in and out of sleep, it was evident from the way everything sounded muffled that something was wrong with my hearing. That I didn't panic seems incredible now. It's just that not only did the nurses and my parents give me the impression that it was just temporary, but I also felt so generally awful that not hearing right was just no big deal at that point. It was enough to awaken and see my parents and sister standing beside my bed. Too weak to really talk, I just drank in little fuzzy things about them that brought an inner smile my lack of energy kept from my lips: the way Mom was wearing my pearl pendant, Dad's quirky eyebrows, and Paige's current hairstyle. Then everything would blur and I would fall asleep again.

"Alison?" I eventually managed to get out, afraid that she might be in a room down the hall. Before I drifted away again, I understood, as through too many woolly caps, that my friend was all right.

I went home in an ambulance, probably a little early since Dad was a physician. My room, after ten days in the hospital, looked like every Christmas and birthday present I had ever had, all rolled into one. I still couldn't walk, and I didn't have enough energy to try the paint-by-number set or even the crossword puzzle book people had given me, so if I wasn't hearing everything, either, it got to me no more than the rest.

What blind faith I had that it would all come back! I even

thought ahead to playing in the piano competition, wearing one of those fall outfits Alison and I had seen at the mall, and although it would probably remain only a fantasy, the perfect date with Jay Cassidy.

That optimism soon began to collide with the fact that my hearing wasn't bouncing back. I mean, after close to three weeks, wasn't it time for this auditory fuzziness to be wearing off? The stronger I grew physically, the more it bothered me, and my mother picked up on it.

I don't know what I would have done without her in the wake of a medical ordeal that had severely weakened me and left me struggling to deal with the life of screwed-up hearing I had been thrust into. She was a dynamo and the driving force behind my filling hours left empty because I wasn't strong enough to do things with friends, in my keeping up with home-work when I was finally ready, and in comforting me when I thought my heart would break. Dad was convinced that she babied me too much, but the truth is, I needed her arms around me frequently; I even needed her to sometimes lie down with me as I fell asleep at night. Just as she had banished my fears of the dark when I was little, her close presence—her being Mommy again—helped still the dawning mixture of hurt, fear, anger, and uncertainty brought on by, first, the realization that even with passing time I couldn't hear right and, then, the knowledge that it was getting worse.

With Dad at work and Paige in school, it was Mom who carried me out to the other room to watch television after I came home from the hospital, and it was she who was there when I found out that I couldn't understand the voices on the screen. Since I hadn't heard human speech normally for weeks, I don't know why I thought the television would be better, but I did.

She propped me up with pillows on the davenport in the family room and flipped it on via remote. It was just one of those simple tasks we do a hundred times and never think much about, but on that day I stopped taking a lot of things for granted.

For a moment, everything seemed all right. After no TV

for weeks, it was good to see the talk show hostess sitting with two guests in the familiar butterscotch-colored leather chairs. Then I realized that I couldn't make out anything they were saying. Was the volume too low? Was it static or something with the local station? I didn't know, but something was very wrong.

"Mom?"

"Let's turn it up a little," I think she said, and she did, but it didn't help. Some sound was there for me, but it was distorted into something unfamiliar and, worse, unintelligible.

I didn't immediately process what was going on. It must be our set, I assumed. Then I entered a transient, otherworldly state as if I were a character in a sci-fi movie who had just passed into a new, weird dimension.

I sat up straighter, sure that I would slip back into the right, normal mode, but it didn't help. This was real. Mom was there in her yellow shorts. The black-and-white-checked drapes were anchors. And I could feel the nubby fabric of the familiar tweed couch. If it wasn't the TV, though, it must be me, and with that realization, panic sizzled through me.

"Mom! I can't understand them. Do something!" She had made everything all right for me for so many years, whether it had been sewing a favorite Raggedy Ann doll's arm back on or taking an orphaned sparrow that was sure to die and somehow healing it.

Her powerlessness to make the television sound right for me must have been wrenching for her, too. I don't remember what she said to me, only that her arms slid around me.

It had been one thing to lie in bed groggily and have voices register hazily, but I was getting a little stronger at that point, and the television experience was the line that marked my realization that something was drastically, maybe even permanently, wrong with my hearing.

I went on full red alert.

—CHAPTER THREE—

Everything "being a blur" is such a trite expression, but it describes my emotions during and right after the funeral. Death at sixteen just shouldn't happen. How do you bury a little sister who would never graduate from high school, never meet someone and fall in love, or marry and have children? There might have been a career. There would have been accomplishments rippling out to touch and better the lives of others. Might have been; would have been: the phrases struck me like an anvil, bespeaking such great loss, such wasted talent and potential, that my living in a blur was, when it came right down to it, all I could manage.

After the blur, though, and after the initial tears, I had to devise a plan of action to stay sane about this, and that hinged upon getting some answers to that maddening, soul-searing question: Why?

Since Mom and Dad were in too deep a state of grief to be questioned about my sister just yet, I turned to others, needing my parents but trying to understand that, except for Dad's arms around me briefly, they seemed to have forgotten that it was my loss, too. "You're the strong one," Aunt Winnie explained.

All I knew was that it had been pills, and as I came out of the fog and life began to focus just a bit, it made less and less sense to me that Abby had taken a deliberate overdose.

A memory surfaced. I had come home at Thanksgiving to find my sister upset. "What's wrong?" I asked. Abby, although quiet, was usually sunbeams and smiles.

"You didn't hear?"

I shook my head.

"Victoria killed herself." There was a stunned puzzlement in Abby's voice. As I felt for my sister, I thought how sad it was for any young life to end that way.

"Victoria Beckman?" Although she hadn't been Abby's close friend, the girls had been classmates since second or third grade, ending up in orchestra together.

Abby confirmed it, and I must have consoled her, but it is my sister's adamant response that rang through my thoughts now: "I could never in a million years do that, Paige."

Never in a million years, never in a million years . . . .

What on earth had motivated my sister?

The first person from whom I sought an answer was our family doctor, who said the amount of medication in Abby's system was inconsistent with accidental overdose. "In other words, Paige, I'm as sure as humanly possible that it was suicide."

Then I tried the specialist the family doctor had told me Abby was seeing, a Dr. Richard Damon, but he was out of town.

I even contacted Greg Miller, an old school friend of mine who was now with the police, and everything was, according to Greg, consistent with taking one's own life.

Never in a million years . . . but the "million years" had come for Abby, and that only renewed my vow to find out why.

I started with Abby's best friend, Alison Wang, who broke into tears at the sight of me. I hadn't seen her since the funeral and felt just as choked up. Alison without Abby was an abomination. For an instant, I saw them as nine-year-olds balancing precariously as aspiring gymnasts on a board stretched between two ladders. The two had clicked in a big way in kindergarten, and it was a friendship that, from all appearances, had continued to grow even through Abby's illness and the resultant changes in her life.

I hugged her now. "Ali, I'm so sorry."

"So am I," she offered. Then, tears finally staunched, her expression changed to something I couldn't quite put my finger on. Could it be some clue as to Abby's state of mind?

"What are you thinking?" I asked.

"Oh, I just keep remembering how dumb I sometimes was. Right from the day Abby got sick, I made so many mistakes, Paige.

se you do. You dropped us off sometimes."

 always seemed happy to be going there," I com-
embering the two lotion-scented girls, beach bags
es in hand, giggling about something that was their
hich I suspected had to do with some hunky boy at
ter having gone through so much, Abby seemed in
ys like any other girl last summer.

 both were. Being at the pool was kind of like old
athered on sunblock and lazed in the sun, frequently
n the pool. We spent time checking out guys and just
u know how Abby did pretty well up close, one-to-
of our favorite things was sitting on the rope—you
ope with the floats on it that separates the deep end
hallow end. We'd sit there watching the swimmers
 our legs a little, and she seemed really comfortable
 You probably remember the regular diving board
h dive."

 dded.

yway, I'd go dive, but Abby just wouldn't. I'm not
really understood," Alison continued, "and Abby didn't
nt to get into it. There were a lot of things, come to
 that she clammed up about."

hink it was an equilibrium problem, Alison. Before
ou are talking about, we went back to Ohio to visit our
nts, and there was a small lake, called a borrow pit, on
erty. It made such a perfect swimming hole that they
red a raft a little way from the shore, and we swam out
off it, and sometimes just sunned ourselves out there.
 it for years, long before Abby got sick. The time I'm
f, though, no one anticipated how her body had been
 her illness, beyond her hearing. She swam out to the
ove off as she had a hundred times in years before, but
 come back up on her own."

h, no."

bby explained later the terror of not knowing which
up and which was down in water grown murky from

Why didn't I pick up on her needs more often or remember when I did know them?"

I shook my head. "I don't know. I've felt the same way." I could have expanded upon my guilt feelings or consoled Abby's friend, but Alison needed to talk, I sensed, and I didn't want to rob her of that opportunity or dilute anything she might say by expressing my own feelings just then. I touched her arm, and she looked at me. "Why don't you tell me about it?"

"It's just little things, I guess."

"Such as?"

"Oh, I dunno. Like the time only a couple of months after she was sick and she still wasn't very strong. You remember how she had so much trouble walking."

"Mmm hmm."

"She was so tired of being cooped up in the house and feeling cut off from things, especially from being with friends. You know, just things we take for granted, like hearing about what's going on, seeing what people are wearing, and just hanging out with the crowd. She once told me that she felt like everybody was moving ahead and she was just standing still.

"Anyway, I don't know whose idea it was for her to try going to the football game, or even if it was a good choice for her social 'coming out,' but she went. Your mom and I talked about it on the phone beforehand. In the end, she dropped us off at the gate early so that I could help Abby on the bleachers before everyone got there, to minimize her feeling of being on-stage and so she wouldn't get bumped. Abby could have settled for the first row, but she determinedly pointed several rows up. Hands clammy from the effort, she struggled and made it. They ought to give medals for that."

Abby's determination had been one of her greatest strengths, and for just a moment when I realized anew that that and all her other qualities had been stilled forever, the weight of loss made it hard to breathe.

Alison continued. "She was so thin, but she looked great that night, like a model. She had her hair sort of turned under in an old-fashioned pageboy, and she wore a new black-and-white tee and some black jeans. I don't know why I remember that, but I do. Even though she couldn't walk easily or hear right, Abby said she felt pretty normal for the first time since she'd been sick. As people poured in and the bleachers filled up, lots of them came over to say hello and tell her how glad they were to see her. I don't think she really heard them, but she got their mood.

"Then the game started, and everybody got caught up in that. It was the usual fun and stuff, which meant scoping people out as much as watching the action, if you know what I mean."

"I remember."

"Even though Abby couldn't stand up each time the Slicers scored, nobody stared at her or seemed to notice that she used her hands to brace herself on the narrow seat. Well, one time I glanced at her, and she wasn't even watching the game or anyone in particular. She was somewhere else, just so obviously savoring being outdoors with people all around and doing something so ordinary. She gave me the most incredible smile."

My own smile was bittersweet. That kind of enjoyment of something so simple was pure Abby.

"Well, toward the end of the game, somebody I knew called for me to come on down a few rows, so I did, and we got to talking. The game ended, and I sort of automatically turned to Abby and motioned for her to join me. Then I talked a little more to this other girl, and she and I started walking down to the ground."

That ashamed look returned to Alison's eyes. "What happened?"

"Oh, Paige. I totally forgot that I was supposed to help Abby down as well as up, and by the time I remembered, I was being swept along with the flow of people leaving. Even then, I thought that Abby must be there in the crowd, like old times, but when I looked back, I saw . . . ."

Her voice broke, and I saw one perfect tear stain her cheek at the memory.

"It's all right, Aliso⌷

"Abby wasn't in ba⌷ bleachers, she was sitting, ⌷ how she would ever get d⌷ must just have been breaki⌷

"But, you know," sh⌷ back of her hand, "Abby ne⌷ acted cold or anything."

I didn't blame Aliso⌷ of how Abby's life had chang⌷ much. Alison, don't be too h⌷ new to Abby was also new to⌷ remembered, I'm sure, eve⌷ bleachers, wasn't that you fo⌷ the sum total of your friends⌷ her even after she was sick. S⌷ the one who came into her⌷ recuperating, sometimes with⌷ sometimes just to listen or be⌷ connected her to her friends ⌷ to school and when she was f⌷ the one who played Yahtzee w⌷ felt she could cry with. But I⌷ wracked with guilt myself for⌷ having been older and sometin⌷ nuisance.

"Alison, the bleacher i⌷ years ago. What had she bee⌷ recently?"

"I didn't know you felt g⌷

"I think we all do to some⌷ Which didn't help me to know, ⌷ feel better.

Alison thought for a few⌷ "It was kind of a jumble of samen⌷ know how we went to the pool⌷

Well, of cou⌷

"She⌷ mented, re⌷ and sunglas⌷ secret and ⌷ the pool. A⌷ so many w⌷

"We⌷ times. We s⌷ cooling off⌷ talking. Yo⌷ one. One⌷ know that ⌷ from the s⌷ and kicking⌷ doing that⌷ and the hi⌷

I n⌷

"A⌷ sure I ever⌷ seem to w⌷ think of it⌷

"I⌷ the time y⌷ grandpare⌷ their prop⌷ had anch⌷ to it, dove⌷ We'd don⌷ thinking ⌷ affected b⌷ raft and d⌷ she didn⌷

way was⌷

Why didn't I pick up on her needs more often or remember when I did know them?"

I shook my head. "I don't know. I've felt the same way." I could have expanded upon my guilt feelings or consoled Abby's friend, but Alison needed to talk, I sensed, and I didn't want to rob her of that opportunity or dilute anything she might say by expressing my own feelings just then. I touched her arm, and she looked at me. "Why don't you tell me about it?"

"It's just little things, I guess."

"Such as?"

"Oh, I dunno. Like the time only a couple of months after she was sick and she still wasn't very strong. You remember how she had so much trouble walking."

"Mmm hmm."

"She was so tired of being cooped up in the house and feeling cut off from things, especially from being with friends. You know, just things we take for granted, like hearing about what's going on, seeing what people are wearing, and just hanging out with the crowd. She once told me that she felt like everybody was moving ahead and she was just standing still.

"Anyway, I don't know whose idea it was for her to try going to the football game, or even if it was a good choice for her social 'coming out,' but she went. Your mom and I talked about it on the phone beforehand. In the end, she dropped us off at the gate early so that I could help Abby on the bleachers before everyone got there, to minimize her feeling of being on-stage and so she wouldn't get bumped. Abby could have settled for the first row, but she determinedly pointed several rows up. Hands clammy from the effort, she struggled and made it. They ought to give medals for that."

Abby's determination had been one of her greatest strengths, and for just a moment when I realized anew that that and all her other qualities had been stilled forever, the weight of loss made it hard to breathe.

Alison continued. "She was so thin, but she looked great that night, like a model. She had her hair sort of turned under in an old-fashioned pageboy, and she wore a new black-and-white tee and some black jeans. I don't know why I remember that, but I do. Even though she couldn't walk easily or hear right, Abby said she felt pretty normal for the first time since she'd been sick. As people poured in and the bleachers filled up, lots of them came over to say hello and tell her how glad they were to see her. I don't think she really heard them, but she got their mood.

"Then the game started, and everybody got caught up in that. It was the usual fun and stuff, which meant scoping people out as much as watching the action, if you know what I mean."

"I remember."

"Even though Abby couldn't stand up each time the Slicers scored, nobody stared at her or seemed to notice that she used her hands to brace herself on the narrow seat. Well, one time I glanced at her, and she wasn't even watching the game or anyone in particular. She was somewhere else, just so obviously savoring being outdoors with people all around and doing something so ordinary. She gave me the most incredible smile."

My own smile was bittersweet. That kind of enjoyment of something so simple was pure Abby.

"Well, toward the end of the game, somebody I knew called for me to come on down a few rows, so I did, and we got to talking. The game ended, and I sort of automatically turned to Abby and motioned for her to join me. Then I talked a little more to this other girl, and she and I started walking down to the ground."

That ashamed look returned to Alison's eyes. "What happened?"

"Oh, Paige. I totally forgot that I was supposed to help Abby down as well as up, and by the time I remembered, I was being swept along with the flow of people leaving. Even then, I thought that Abby must be there in the crowd, like old times, but when I looked back, I saw . . . ."

Her voice broke, and I saw one perfect tear stain her cheek at the memory.

"It's all right, Alison. What did you see?"

"Abby wasn't in back of me at all. There, all alone in the bleachers, she was sitting, just waiting and probably wondering how she would ever get down on her own. I knew her heart must just have been breaking. I felt like such a crud.

"But, you know," she said, wiping away the tear with the back of her hand, "Abby never blamed me, never scolded me or acted cold or anything."

I didn't blame Alison, either, but the one small instance of how Abby's life had changed cut into me. "She didn't complain much. Alison, don't be too hard on yourself. Everything that was new to Abby was also new to the rest of us. What Abby knew and remembered, I'm sure, even when she was stranded on the bleachers, wasn't that you forgot she needed your help. It was the sum total of your friendship and the way you stood beside her even after she was sick. She no doubt recalled that you were the one who came into her bedroom regularly when she was recuperating, sometimes with books, other times with news, and sometimes just to listen or be listened to. You were the one who connected her to her friends when she was too weak to go back to school and when she was forgotten by so many of the others, the one who played Yahtzee with her for hours, and the one she felt she could cry with. But I know how you feel, because I'm wracked with guilt myself for having been away at college, for having been older and sometimes thinking my little sister was a nuisance.

"Alison, the bleacher incident happened a couple of years ago. What had she been like this past year, especially recently?"

"I didn't know you felt guilty, too."

"I think we all do to some extent in this kind of situation." Which didn't help me to know, but maybe it would make Alison feel better.

Alison thought for a few moments about my question. "It was kind of a jumble of sameness and difference. I mean, you know how we went to the pool almost every day last summer.

Well, of course you do. You dropped us off sometimes."

"She always seemed happy to be going there," I commented, remembering the two lotion-scented girls, beach bags
and sunglasses in hand, giggling about something that was their
secret and which I suspected had to do with some hunky boy at
the pool. After having gone through so much, Abby seemed in
so many ways like any other girl last summer.

"We both were. Being at the pool was kind of like old
times. We slathered on sunblock and lazed in the sun, frequently
cooling off in the pool. We spent time checking out guys and just
talking. You know how Abby did pretty well up close, one-to-
one. One of our favorite things was sitting on the rope—you
know that rope with the floats on it that separates the deep end
from the shallow end. We'd sit there watching the swimmers
and kicking our legs a little, and she seemed really comfortable
doing that. You probably remember the regular diving board
and the high dive."

I nodded.

"Anyway, I'd go dive, but Abby just wouldn't. I'm not
sure I ever really understood," Alison continued, "and Abby didn't
seem to want to get into it. There were a lot of things, come to
think of it, that she clammed up about."

"I think it was an equilibrium problem, Alison. Before
the time you are talking about, we went back to Ohio to visit our
grandparents, and there was a small lake, called a borrow pit, on
their property. It made such a perfect swimming hole that they
had anchored a raft a little way from the shore, and we swam out
to it, dove off it, and sometimes just sunned ourselves out there.
We'd done it for years, long before Abby got sick. The time I'm
thinking of, though, no one anticipated how her body had been
affected by her illness, beyond her hearing. She swam out to the
raft and dove off as she had a hundred times in years before, but
she didn't come back up on her own."

"Oh, no."

"Abby explained later the terror of not knowing which
way was up and which was down in water grown murky from

the mud we had stirred up with our paddling. As she described it, almost out of air, she thought she was frantically clawing toward the surface, but, Alison, she was going the wrong way, straight to the bottom. Her sense of direction was off."

"That's terrible. What happened?"

"A quick-thinking cousin noticed her absence, figured it out, and pulled her up. So, that's why she avoided the diving board at the pool."

"I wonder why she didn't tell me."

I did, too. "Maybe she just didn't want to break the spell of the fun at the pool by putting into words what she could no longer do."

"Yeah, maybe. Anyway, to get back to my story, there was this lifeguard, John Sperati, last summer, and he was really cool. He had that Italian *something*, and when he smiled, his teeth blazed like a toothpaste ad. He was about seventeen to our fifteen, and he was from another school, which made him sort of mysterious. Anyway, everyone showed off to get his attention, but do you know who it was he liked?"

"My sister?"

"Right on. She looked older in her swimsuit, and he'd stand over us when we were in the water . . . you know . . . hanging onto the edge of the pool. He liked to joke around, but he was serious when he asked Abby out."

"I didn't know that."

"Well, it almost didn't work out. He was standing above us, and some children were splashing and shouting, and Abby didn't hear him right."

"What happened?"

"When she didn't get what he said, she deferred to me. She told him, 'You'll have to ask Alison.' Well, he just roared with laughter."

"Oh, no!" I recalled how we had relayed information to her, and I also remembered myself at that age, sensitive and unsure of myself, especially around guys. It must have been terribly embarrassing.

"John thought it was hilarious and made a big thing about Abby needing my permission to go out on a date. It might have been funny, but Abby was so mortified that her hearing had failed at a time like that. After she knew what was going on and told him that she'd have to ask her parents and would let him know, after he was gone, she cried her eyes out in the locker room. It wasn't so much that she had wanted to go. It's that she felt like such a fool, a freak, like such a dud, she told me.

"So, even though it was a good summer in many ways, her not hearing right certainly messed things up sometimes, Paige, and it snowballed as the school year started and went along."

And I'd been away at college, oblivious. I sighed. I couldn't do anything about that now. "Could you give me some examples?"

"Well, for one thing, she tried hard with the hearing aid, and it was making life miserable for her, since it didn't bring in the kind of sound she needed. Some of the teachers didn't understand why Abby turned it off during class, either. You know, stuff like, 'Abby, don't you want to hear?' or 'Abby isn't cooperating.' There was lots of negative attention, and it was just basically a bad rap here and a bad rap there."

It was then, I think, that I began wondering what a day in my sister's school life had been like. I was about to probe when Alison started speaking again.

"It wasn't all that bad, though. There was Mr. Jeffers for comp. We all thought he was too old-time. He liked memorization, he made us pay a dime each time we said yeah or anything else he thought was slang, and he was a stickler for accurate spelling and grammar. But he couldn't have been nicer or more sensitive to Abby."

I really wanted to understand this. "In what ways?"

"Let me think. Well, he gave us a list of ten or twelve new vocabulary words each and every Monday that we had to spell right and use in a sentence. Everybody groaned. They were hard words that he liked to clump together alphabetically, like one 'O' series: *obfuscate, oscillate, obdurate,* etc."

When Alison rolled her eyes, I said, "Those do sound tricky."

"It was even worse because he never told us when he would test us on them. It could be several days later or the very next day, so we had to learn them all that first night. Anyway, I found out from Abby that he talked to her one day after school and suggested that she memorize exactly which words were on each list, so that when he called them off orally for the quiz, she could just write them in any order and not have to worry about hearing or lipreading them in the right sequence. Some of them, like the ones on that 'O' list, looked or sounded the same to Abby, she said, so this was a big relief to her. But no one knew. Mr. Jeffers did it quietly and didn't embarrass her in front of everyone like some teachers did.

"I remember this once, for instance, our biology teacher was really into spelling bees to help us keep the scientific terminology straight. You know, stuff like *lepidoptera* and *hymenoptera*. As you can probably imagine, that was murder for Abby. You know as well as I do that she was a crack speller, but she just didn't hear, Paige, and this witch of a teacher actually eliminated her if she spelled the wrong word, even if she spelled it correctly, or—get this—even if she asked to have it repeated. Can you imagine? I mean, she just never budged, never gave Abby a second chance or tried to look directly at her when she pronounced each word, and there were days when Abby was sick to her stomach before those classes. Poor Abby. If it wasn't enough to be unfairly disqualified from the bee, the teacher would make a huge thing of it: 'Abby, I don't know why you don't listen better.'"

I shook my head, sick at the thought of my sister being ridiculed by someone in authority, someone who, with all the new laws and awareness, should have known how to deal with someone with diminished hearing. Or, no, it went even beyond that; it came down to human empathy, regardless of laws, politics, and school policies. "Thank goodness for the Mr. Jefferses of the world. Alison, did my parents know about the biology spelling bees?"

"No, I don't think so."

"Whyever not?"

"Abby didn't want your mom to go to the teacher and make a thing about it, and she didn't want to tell anyone else, because she didn't want them to, as she put it, `sic' an interpreter or special education on her. So, she just brazened it out. Do you think that was wrong?"

"Not necessarily, but it makes me angry at the teacher, and it makes me ache for Abby's having had to deal with tripe like that. Did that kind of thing happen very often?"

"I didn't have that many classes with her, and as you said, she didn't complain a whole lot, so I don't really know.

"As the year went on, she got more and more unhappy. I know she wanted to ditch the hearing aid and just try to read lips without the interference. When she was with me, she could do it really well, you know, but the teachers seemed to catch on when she turned it off, and they sometimes came down on her.

"I got wrapped up in my music, practicing my piece for the Young Artists' Competition."

Alison played the violin. "I heard that congratulations are in order."

"Thanks, but I didn't take first."

"It's an honor, though, just to make the finals. You play like an angel."

I was surprised to see her eyes mist over. "That's what people said about Abby and the piano," she explained. "Abby didn't begrudge the fact that I still did those things, but I know it tore her heart out not to be readying herself for competition, too, as she once had, and it changed our friendship just a little. I mean, we used to go to orchestra together and practice together. We talked music, music, music. That special thread of our friendship was pulled away when she got sick, and the others never meshed together quite right to hide the rip. We were still friends, but something had changed.

"I hardly saw her outside of school the last couple of

months. I heard Jay Cassidy asked her out and she turned him down, and I went over to your house. I mean, Abby turning down Jay? She told me once that just getting a glimpse of him in the halls made things like the biology spelling bee bearable. He was her dream date. I was going to try to find out what was going on and make an attempt to get her to change her mind."

"And did you?"

"No. She was like a different person that day, all shut inside herself. If you want to know about that time, ask Mark Friedell."

The name rang a bell, but I wasn't sure why. "Mark Friedell?"

"He's a teacher, and Abby started going to his house sometimes after school. She wouldn't talk about it. Why, oh, why, didn't I see it coming, Paige?"

"None of us did, sweetheart."

"Why did she do this to us?"

"Do you mean to leave us?"

She shook her head, jaw clenched. "Yeah, and leave us wondering, blaming ourselves for seeing such a beautiful life just wasted. Wasted, Paige. I feel so mad sometimes, but I don't know if it's more at her or myself.

"You know, I'm all talked out."

Anger, guilt, supreme sadness: legacies of survivorship. I said a few words, at a loss to really comfort Abby's best friend or give her the answers she needed. I hugged her again. We promised to keep in touch.

Then I left.

⸺CHAPTER FOUR⸺

Abby *Aaah-aaah-aaah!* I erupted like a banshee in the shower in an attempt to pop that imaginary sound barrier. When even my blood-curdling scream sounded faraway, though, it just scraped at that new raw place deep within me. Why me? What had I done? I couldn't hear; I couldn't hear! Would I smother in the absence of normal sound, or did it just feel that way?

Even the shower brought no escape, since the water rushing into one ear made no sound at all and a distorted noise in the other. Couldn't I even have that bit of the way it used to be?

For a moment as I sniffed Paige's favorite citron-scented shampoo, I felt little again, and safe. "There, it's all right," my sister had said any number of times, whether it was in pulling out a splinter with the tweezers or banishing an imaginary bogeyman from under my bed.

Missing her, I lathered in her shampoo and for a moment saw us dressed entirely in black on Halloween. Paige had never thought of herself as having many talents beyond her natural athleticism, but she could do so much, including whip up anything with a needle. The year I was six, instead of buying or renting us costumes for a community party, she had taken a remnant of black felt for ears, some yarn to braid into tails, and ribbon that, along with eyebrow pencil whiskers, had transformed us into matching black cats. We had won first place in the pairs category.

Crunching leaves underfoot, we had proudly strolled home hand-in-hand, only to find our carefully carved jack-o'-lantern smashed.

"Why, Paige?"

"I don't know, Abby." Her honesty, if not her ability to fix my pumpkin, had soothed me.

In contrast, I felt so alone now, and scared. That had been just a pumpkin, only for one Halloween, and these were my ears. Would it be forever?

In the shower, tears mingled with spray, I looked down. Water and soap eddied at the drain. All gone: the safety was all gone, and the water spiraling down might just as well have been my old, familiar life.

"*Uh ooo i mmm ooo,*" Mom cheerily said one day as she breezed into my room in her favorite aqua slacks. I was still too weak to walk much, so I spent a lot of time in bed, where I kept busy, if you can call it that, doing things such as reading historical novels.

"Huh?" I heard better on some days than on others, so that what I received ranged widely from whole sentences, to ooos and uhs, on down to major gaps. Today was one of the days I heard but didn't really hear, and the jump from the romance of the French Court in my book to the reality of still another mangled sentence brought me crashing back to what my life had become.

A bowl of tomato soup on a tray next to a sandwich with the crust cut off clued me in. *Would you like some soup?* Yeah, that must have been it. How could such a simple question be so hard to get? Tomato soup? Right then, what I wanted was to throw the steaming red liquid at the wall.

And so it went.

To sleep was to blot everything out. For just one little minute as I woke up, lost in that region between slumber and wakefulness, I had the illusion that everything was all right. Then something that should have made a certain sound wouldn't register, and I had to learn to live in my altered state all over again. My heart broke every single day.

So, of course, I was as desperate for medical help as my parents were, ready for anything to restore my hearing and get me out of the stifling rabbit hole I had fallen into. I submitted to a vast array of hearing tests (we learned that one ear was dead and probably had been from the time of my coma) and medical exams. My father, a dermatologist, had faith in drugs, which is probably why we grasped at medication as a way to help, but nothing worked: not the pills that changed my voice to a squeak and made me feel as if someone were strangling me; not the one that gave me an itchy rash and made me vomit; and certainly not the one that made my skin burn as if thousands of tiny needles were pricking it. There were steroids and even a vitamin therapy that made my breath smell like rising dough every time I opened my mouth. "Wonder Girl" a few people called me, after the bread.

We weren't very far into trying these possibilities when about a month after I got sick, Paige returned to school, Alison went back—everyone did but me. It was a lot more than my hearing that kept me from going into ninth grade on time; I just wasn't getting my strength back very fast, my balance was off, and I needed to sleep long hours. I was too tired at that point, and too filled with a combination of unreality, fear, and frustration, to even feel that left out.

When I was strong enough, my mother brought home assignments for, at first, just one class, English, and although I didn't have any trouble choosing *lie* or *lay* as the right verb, just doing one simple exercise felt like an uphill jog. My handwriting was as stiff as my post-meningitis walk, and it was a major feat to stay propped up in a writing position for very long. Dad even bought me a nice, new laptop, which I couldn't use because my eyes had become supersensitive to light and certain rapid motions. The illness had changed my body in a lot of ways, if only temporarily in some cases.

Even if my hearing wasn't improving, and although I sometimes had those weird side effects from the medications, I did gradually get stronger, and it wasn't long before we added a second academic subject and then a third.

Alison was great, coming over often, except . . . well . . . I just couldn't help longing for the easy way it used to be with her when I didn't have to struggle for every little crumb. It was that same yo-yo deal where sometimes I could understand most of what she said and other times it was hit-or-miss. Even though I appreciated the way she tried so hard, and even wrote things down when I was having a bad day, it was that extra effort on her part that made us unequal and somehow changed our friendship just a bit.

Of course I didn't just waltz back in when it was finally time to go back to school part-time. Mom had talked to the right people when I wasn't strong enough to return on schedule, and with their cooperation, I was proud of having kept up at home. Current homework in hand, I thought I was ready, right down to the new lightweight sweater in my favorite periwinkle blue.

Ready? That was a laugh. It was a good hearing day, but from the moment I entered the building, the scene was kind of surreal, like that old, standard nightmare some people have about being out in public without some essential piece of clothing. I felt so exposed. Right there in the halls before I ever made it to the classroom, I sensed a hush as I passed, stares as if I were some rare zoo animal, and comments that ranged from "You don't look that bad" to "We heard you were in a nursing home." One guy actually said, "Oh, you're not dead." Naturally, I had to strain to get these gems.

In fact, it took me only about thirty seconds to realize the chasm between listening to Paige or Alison one-on-one in my bedroom and being thrust into this new situation with scores of voices that blurred together like a combination Gregorian chant and air conditioner hum; certain laughs or yells punctuated the din like diesel horn blasts, and I almost hurt from listening.

I tried to compensate when I could by being the one to talk, but I quickly learned that without hearing my own voice as I once had, my volume control was off. "Speak up!" went the refrain, which only made me so self-conscious that I piped way down.

Too many old friends hovered, and I found out fast by

the way some of the others looked away or otherwise avoided me that they had become ex-friends. Did they think not hearing right was contagious? Was I too much trouble? A precious few, like Alison, treated me like me.

"Abby's coming out of her shell," my sixth grade teacher had written on my report card. It was funny. I had always liked the learning part of school and the thrill of new workbooks and long pencils with still-perfect erasers, but looking back, it's evident that I must have been paralyzingly shy almost from the start. I don't know if people are born shy or become that way, but whatever the answer, I just was. Even when I knew the reply to a question in fourth grade, for instance, I just didn't want to raise my hand and have all those eyes boring into me. I sat there, instead, like a little sponge soaking up information and contributing what I could through a special symbiosis with my teachers, who liked my quietness and punctuality. I made my workbook pages as perfect as I could, and heart beating three times its normal rate, I answered politely when called upon.

Time eased that kind of stage fright, but from the first day back at school after my sickness, I felt like that little fourth-grader again, wishing I could bury my face into Emma's familiar, safe softness.

Strength still not back to normal, I began with a single class. Mrs. Bennett had a big Welcome Back speech, most of which I heard because I sat up front, but that didn't keep me from turning nineteen shades of red when she went on and on, repeatedly using the word *courage*. Courage? She meant well, but I was just doing what I had to, wasn't I?

She just wouldn't let it go. In announcing a new assignment, an essay on great composers, she shook her head sympathetically and said right there in front of the whole class, "We feel for you, Abby. I can't imagine not hearing music anymore, can you, class?"

Little cold prickles of gooseflesh erupted all over my body, and I was too embarrassed by the unwanted attention to look around to see if everyone nodded their heads. I didn't want pity! It was bad enough in my private heart of hearts to miss normal-sounding music almost more than anything else.

Change the subject, I silently pleaded with Mrs. Bennett, but when she spoke again, it got even worse.

"That's why I'm assigning you your choice of European artists as a topic instead, Abby."

I smiled, sick inside. The deed had been done and trumpeted. What had my mother said to her, anyway? Why would she think that my interest in music had vanished along with my ability to hear perfectly? I didn't know, but the gooseflesh internalized into a hot coal of anger. Writing a paper on a composer, after all, didn't involve listening, only reading about him or her and writing an essay, which was right up my alley. Couldn't I still have my music, still at least write on Beethoven or Rachmaninoff even if significant portions of their compositions were lost to me as sound?

But what got me even more was how, although well-intentioned, Mrs. Bennett hadn't even asked me if I wanted a waiver. She hadn't stopped to consider that I might be more comfortable doing the same assignment as everyone else. In singling me out, in ironically trying to "spare" me, she had defeated her purpose by disregarding my needs in a way that made me feel even more different, more isolated, than I needed to be.

And so it went.

With time, as I added another class and then still another, as hard as it was, I forced myself to speak out. In the beginning, though, when the strangeness of my hearing loss in relation to school was still a shock, I just went with the flow, which sometimes carried me into currents that threatened to drown me.

Except for a few teachers who instinctively knew what to do, or who learned well, even the nice ones tended to overdo it. "Are you getting this, Abby?" Mr. Toler asked me time and again as a class sidebar. Everybody loved Mr. Toler, and I think he really cared, but then again, I wasn't positive it was a real question. I mean, we often ask how people are but don't necessarily want a detailed description or an abrupt "Lousy." It would have taken a speech on "holes" to explain what I was getting and what I missed. Odd: he never asked except right in the middle of discussions. The really good teachers asked me things like that in private, but the catch was that I wasn't sure yet exactly what it was that I needed, except just to be me, to learn, and to be as much like everyone else as possible.

As for the bits and pieces, if I had thought they were murder to put together at home, they multiplied in number and complexity at school. Every teacher had about two dozen other students to watch and listen to: to educate. I didn't want to be singled out, but it helped when they quietly remembered I was there. Each of them had idiosyncrasies that sometimes cut into my reception of their speech, but often all it took was being looked at for me to understand. There were the room pacers, there was one who sat on the edge of her desk and examined her fingernails half the time, and others with a propensity for talking to the chalkboard. As time went by, I came into contact with ever-more little quirks: the voice that trailed off at the ends of sentences, the bushy mustache that seemed to soak up sound and sabotage lips so that I couldn't see them, and voices that just didn't register well even on my better hearing days.

Unfortunately, there were a lot of days that were really bad, when every other word seemed to be a blank; on those, I went home drained from the strain of listening. How could something so simple have become so complex?

To make it worse, people could be so dense: "You mean you didn't hear *that*?" "It's too bad you are going to forget how to talk." "Speak up, Abby." "Don't interrupt, Abby." On and on it went.

So going back to school was like watching television at home for the first time after my illness and realizing that it would never be the same. The tough part was, there was no privacy, no mother to put her arms around me, no closed-captions to bail me out this time, and no avoidance of being thrust into the spotlight of being different.

⟿Chapter Five↼

Mark Friedell answered his door on my second knock. A teacher, Alison had said he was. His shiny hair just missed being black, and the eyes that met mine looked like bittersweet chocolate. Something was there in the eyes: a certain mood. I remembered now who he was, but that didn't explain why Abby had been going to his house or why he seemed—I suddenly discerned that look—eaten up inside. That alone made me glad I had come, wild-goose chase though it might be.

I felt so shut out at home. Dad was buried in his dermatology practice and medical journals, while Mom stayed in their room most of the time, dozing or tearfully poring over old albums. I brought her cups of coffee. I plumped her pillows. I tried to talk in ways I thought would comfort her, and myself, but she was Abby's mother just then, rather than mine, and I guessed she had to deal with the loss in her own way. Seeking answers was mine.

"Paige?" Surprise creased Mark's forehead.

"I saw you at the funeral," I said. The ball had to be in his court. I couldn't come out and accuse him of playing a role, no matter how slight, in my sister's death, but neither could I just let this drop. I had to know what had propelled Abby to violate her beliefs, and maybe this man held some answers.

His dark eyes brushed mine as he ushered me into the living room. "I'm sorry we had to meet again under such circumstances," he said as we sat down.

"No sorrier than I."

The grand piano dominating the room claimed my attention then, and images of my sister, short legs barely reaching the pedals, swirled almost dizzyingly before me. Sometimes it had been my job to walk Abby to her music teacher's, and occasionally I had stayed and listened to her play in this very house for Mark's grandmother, known fondly by her pupils as Madame Marek.

It always amazed me. The little girl who was too timid to recite her lines in the school play had come to life before the piano as, self-consciousness forgotten, a certain brilliance radiated from her spirit, through her fingers, and out as beautiful sound. I wondered if playing the piano was the happiest Abby had ever been. Tears welled at that thought, and Mark Friedell must have seen them.

I did that a lot now, drifting into reveries. He leaned closer to me from his end of the davenport. "Are you all right?"

"Yes. No. Oh, I don't know."

"Again, I can't tell you how sorry I am. You were remembering your sister just then, weren't you? I heard her play, you know."

"Recently?"

"Yes."

I was hungry for information. "Would you be able to tell me about it?"

He nodded, and I listened carefully as he related how he had found my sister in tears before the piano in the school music room. When he had learned that her piano was gone and remembered her skill, he had offered her the instrument that had been his grandmother's and which Abby had played so many times as a child. Arthritis, he explained, had crippled Madame Marek's fingers to the point where she had given up playing and moved to a drier climate. She had left her piano to her grandson who, himself, had become a musician, and he was buying her Cape Cod cottage.

"Abby seemed so . . . so needy, Paige."

"And did she play?"

"Oh, yes."

"How did it affect her?"

"Actually, I made myself scarce, sensing that she needed some privacy to get back into it, but of course I heard her a few times. Taskmistress that she was, Grandmother might have faulted Abby, but it sounded competent to me—no, inspired, fraught with emotion that yanked at my soul. Abby was obviously very moved to be playing again."

I wasn't sure I understood this. I was away at school when my parents had sold the piano that had been such a center of Abby's life, and nothing much had ever been said about it by either them or Abby. I had assumed that my sister, not hearing as before, felt uncomfortable seeing it there, but now I wondered.

"I never really understood why my parents sold our piano."

He shook his head. "It hurt your sister deeply. As she described it to me, the piano was just gone one day."

"Gone? Do you mean that they never talked to her about it first?" That seemed incredible to me. My parents weren't a couple of ogres. In fact, in my memory, they had done everything to support Abby, everything to ease her transition.

"I'm almost positive they didn't," he said.

I could see the disapproval in his expression, and I felt a rush of defensiveness. "They must have had a good reason."

"I agree, but apparently Abby didn't see it, didn't understand it, and I hope I didn't complicate her life by offering her this piano to play."

"I think I understand," I said, but I wondered if playing again had contributed negatively toward her emotional state, and I wasn't sure I liked the idea of his intervention.

"Do you?"

"Did my parents know she was coming here to play?"

He looked at a rose medallion in the area rug. "No."

"Abby didn't tell them?" What reason could she have had? Was there something to hide, after all? I became aware of the contrast between the skinny teenager Mark had been and the mustached, virile man he was now. I had changed less, I thought, although my cheerleader's ponytail was gone.

"'I think she would have, but keep in mind that she felt they had betrayed her by selling her piano. I know they must have thought they had her best interest in mind when they did that. Abby knew it, too, and it's because she did that she worried they would forbid her coming here to play. She didn't want to give up the piano yet again."

"But what could they possibly have had against her playing?"

"You'll have to ask them. Maybe they assumed that she could no longer enjoy it or that playing was clinging to the past. I don't know. My role was to let her play and let her talk, not to grill her."

I wanted to ask if he was sure that was all, but I didn't. "Do you think she was bitter?"

"Bitter? No, I don't. I think it was more that she was reeling from a life that seemed to be spinning out of control. She was more frustrated and bewildered than anything else."

"And depressed."

"Situationally maybe, but you will have to agree that she had good reason to be down about some things. I can't imagine losing my hearing and having my world turned topsy-turvy. It's no small thing. At the same time, Abby didn't want the world to revolve around the fact that her hearing was down, and with all the emphasis some key people in her life placed upon the need to hear, she was stressed. I think it was depersonalizing her."

"They had to, Mark. They couldn't just say, 'Oh, sweetie, you can't hear now' and leave it at that, for Pete's sake."

"I know, but there have to be parameters to help, or 'help' can become a hindrance to persevering and rising above it: to living."

"So, you're saying that they went too far? How can you say that? I mean, if it were me, I would have wanted them to do everything in their power to keep me hearing, keep me normal."

"Maybe you think you would. I did, too, until I talked to your sister at some length, but what it boils down to is that to her, 'normal' had become not hearing. Paige, she felt the others were making her handicapped by ignoring her as a whole person; that is, by letting the disability take the front seat. To Abby's credit, she was becoming more than the girl who didn't hear right. She was moving on, and I think resuming playing reunified her with her strengths enough to help her overcome her limitations, or at least to move in that direction."

Moving on? To what? Suicide? "That doesn't sound like someone who would kill herself."

Mark had that "eaten up" look again. It didn't jibe with what he had just told me, nor did suicide, and I was on the verge of probing when the doorbell rang.

What an inopportune moment! He looked at me apologetically. "Excuse me."

I felt that we were on the edge of something important, and I hoped that Mark would just send the caller away. I couldn't shake the feeling that he knew something about Abby. But what?

The buzz of conversation grew more distinct, and I felt my heart sink as Mark reentered the room with a man about his own age.

"Paige Jensen, this is Will Kricilek. We moonlight together at the Heathman. Will plays a mean sax. In fact, tonight is our night."

Will and I exchanged greetings. A sax? At that point, I didn't care if they played tubas or the zither, but by the way Will looked at his watch, I knew it was time for me to leave.

"I'll be on my way," I said. "I hope it's a good evening. It was nice to meet you, Will. Mark, thanks for your time."

"Come and listen to us some Tuesday," Will suggested as I turned to leave.

"I'll do that."

I glanced at the piano again, swallowed a lump in my throat, and walked toward the door.

"We'll talk more later," Mark assured me as he held it open for me.

I crossed the threshold and gave him a little wave without turning back. *You bet we will!* I thought.

My destination on the college campus had the look of an English cottage, right down to an uneven slate roof and ivy growing over the aged brick. Abby would have loved it. Since its sign read Special Education: Deaf and Hard of Hearing, I knew I was in the right place.

I hadn't gotten very far with Alison or Mark Friedell, and heaven knew that my parents weren't much help, but the maddening "Why?" persisted, and I couldn't just sit around doing nothing to try to understand. Maybe I needed a different approach. It was with the idea that some impartial information on deafness might give me a clue that I had made an appointment with an expert.

I had to wait in the reception area for only a short time before a tall man of about sixty with salt-and-pepper hair walked out. "Hi. I'm Dr. Black," he introduced himself as I stood up.

"Thank you for seeing me on such short notice, Dr. Black. I'm Paige Jensen."

"Come on back to my office."

It was a cubicle that might have seemed depressingly small if it hadn't featured several leaded-glass windows and striking black-and-white photographs of European castles and cathedrals on the walls. As he motioned for me to sit down, I noticed books and stacks of papers everywhere, including the chair where I was supposed to sit.

He laughed good-naturedly as he swept them off. "I'm sorry this room is such a mess. We moved here from another building recently. How may I help you, Paige?"

"Janet Logan, a special education teacher at the high school my sister attended, gave me your name as someone who might be able to help me. I'm looking for some information about deafness."

"That's a big topic. Are there certain areas you want to talk about?"

"Yes." I hesitated for a moment, unsure of how to say it. Then I blundered ahead. "My sixteen-year-old sister, who was deaf . . . well . . . she committed suicide not long ago, and I'm looking for anything, any crumb at all, that might help me to understand what happened. I keep going back in my mind to the idea that her deafness brought it on."

He said what everybody did, although I know that didn't make people insincere. "I can't tell you how sorry I am to hear about your sister. I'm sure that I would also want a better understanding if I were in your shoes. One thing I can tell you is that deaf people do not commit suicide in any greater numbers than would be found in the general population. There are a lot of variables that influence how a person handles deafness, however. Why don't you fill me in a little about your sister's background, such as how and when she became deaf, and how severe her hearing loss was. We can proceed from there."

The wisdom in the eyes behind the glasses, coupled with the sincerity in his voice, made it easier to talk. "Abby had normal hearing until she had meningitis just around her fourteenth birthday. I don't know much about decibel levels and things like that, but I can tell you that it just gradually got worse over the next two years, until there was very little hearing left when she died. Her hearing had gone up and down. For a while, she had a lot of comparatively 'good hearing days,' as she called them, but the ratio of bad to good had really been changing this past year, until almost all her days had become 'bad hearing days.' She wore a hearing aid in the one ear that still had some hearing, but it didn't help much. In fact, she often got upset about wearing it."

"I can understand that. A hearing aid simply makes things louder and doesn't necessarily bring in quality sound. Your sister had a lot to deal with, Paige, especially since this began at an age when so many other physical and emotional changes occur."

"Quality of sound? I thought it was just a matter of volume."

"Unfortunately, no. Fidelity is crucial, especially in comprehending the human voice and in the enjoyment and utilization of the sounds around us. Think of the elaborate sound systems we use to listen to CDs or other recorded sound. Quality is what it's all about."

He turned around and plucked something off a shelf. I

took it when he handed it to me.

"This is a hearing aid microphone," he explained. "You can see that it is only the size of a small pea, so the quality of the sound it produces is very limited, and how much a person profits from the hearing aid varies with the type and degree of hearing loss."

I handed the microphone back to him and nodded. "Maybe that's why Abby sometimes said that she heard but didn't hear." I had the sudden mental picture of her, hands clamped over her ears to shut out the strains of her once-favorite Christmas carol, *Angels We Have Heard on High*, and my voice was husky when I spoke again. "It was especially difficult for her when it came to music. Dr. Black, she was an accomplished pianist before she got sick, playing in competitions and even winning sometimes, and she listened to the radio and old recordings all the time, but music . . . well, it must be the kind of fidelity you were talking about. It had become noise to her, I think. *Noise.*"

"That would have given her a lot to adjust to, especially since she must also have been missing speech along with the music. If there is a distortion, a hearing aid makes it more pronounced. It is not unusual for a person in such a situation to feel very isolated, and it's compounded by deficits in other people's attitudes."

"She did lose some friends when she could no longer participate in the ways she once did, and I can remember it seeming to cut to the quick. Fortunately, others were loyal."

He nodded. "Peer acceptance is certainly an important part of it, but the attitudes of parents, teachers, educational support personnel, and the medical profession also play a significant role. How the parents handle the child's deafness shapes the child's attitude about it, her coping skills, and self-image. If the parents accept the deafness and focus upon the child as an individual who happens to be deaf, instead of on the deafness as something negative that needs to be fixed, it plays a distinctly positive role in the child's development.

"Unfortunately, sometimes parents become so fixated on the deafness and the perceived importance of their child hearing that they forget the child. I can't fault the parents for this. It's more a matter of their not having been provided by professionals with the proper perspective.

"Generally speaking, there tends to be too much emphasis upon hearing technology: hearing aids, cochlear implants, and other ways to foster hearing. Sometimes very well-meaning medical intervention, for example, becomes detrimental to the child's emotional and social welfare and health, since feelings all too often are ignored. Educators and audiologists manage all too often to turn a human being into a set of big ears."

"I had no idea it was so complex."

"It really is. You mentioned Janet Logan. She graduated from my program about ten years ago. Was Abby taking special education classes?"

"No. I was referred to Ms. Logan by a friend. Abby was in regular classes. Did she do something wrong by not taking special classes?"

"Maybe, or maybe not. We have to avoid the cookie cutter mentality that says if special classes are right for one deaf student, then they are right for another. Each has his or her own very specialized needs influenced by variables including the age of onset of deafness, communication mode, and whether or not the child has disabilities in addition to deafness. Many students do just fine in regular classes, while others thrive in special classes or a combination of regular and special.

"A few years ago, I was called over to a school to evaluate a fifteen-year-old girl with a significant hearing loss who was taking regular classes and just not getting by. Her speechreading skills were poor, she didn't sign, and she wasn't assertive enough to feel comfortable asking another student to take notes. So, she missed a lot, and her grades were suffering. In addition, she was becoming withdrawn. When the girl finally began signing and started going to a special school, she blossomed to the extent that she went on to a college for the deaf and forged a career.

"My wife, on the other hand, is also deaf. In fact, she lost her hearing around the time your sister did. My wife was in high school before mainstreaming, but she did just fine in regular classes and has two college degrees. My sister, meanwhile, was born deaf, attended schools for the deaf, and is a respected businesswoman, so it all depends, Paige.

"How did Abby do in school?"

"From the standpoint of grades, she was near the top. I'm in college in the Midwest, so I missed the day-to-day details of it, but I know she diligently applied herself and looked for ways to keep up, such as through extra reading and using the Internet. But I don't know," I added, shocked by my own lack of knowledge, "how Abby felt about school. I just wish I knew so much more."

"You know, I can think of someone who might be able to fill you in much better than I can, and that's my wife, Melissa. Would you be interested in talking to her? Even though no two deaf individuals are alike, I have a hunch she might be able to cast some light onto your sister's situation in ways that I cannot."

"I'd really like that." I didn't think Dr. Black had mentioned his wife as a way of wrapping up our appointment, but I was also aware of the time. "You have given me a lot of food for thought, Dr. Black."

He saw me glance at my watch. I knew from his receptionist that he had a three o'clock class. "Oh, is it that time already?"

There was something about the way he hadn't realized that we had been talking for close to an hour that almost endeared him to me.

Later, I tried to merge the impressions of Abby and of deafness I had been getting, but like pebbles on the shore, they had no clear pattern, and I knew I had to keep looking.

–Chapter Six–

Abby *I was at Alison's in her long, narrow family room with its French doors and hardwood floors. The furniture had been pushed to the edges, and we were all there, dancing and having fun. I heard her parents' old Johnny Mathis rendition of Chances Are perfectly, and my eyes strayed across the room with a longing new to me.*

"He's looking at you," Sarah Randolph whispered. It was the weirdest, most wonderful thing; I understood every word even over the music, just as I had all evening.

Alison strolled up. "How about another soda?"

"Thanks, but not now," I replied automatically, not fully conscious that I had also heard her tiny voice in the noise-filled room, even deafened as I was by the pitter-pat of my heart.

She followed Sarah's and my gaze and grinned. "Oh, I get it. Hey, he's coming over this way."

As my friends melted away, Jay Cassidy strode dreamlike, closer and closer, and I was glad that I had worn something floaty, because the breeze came through the French doors and ruffled my skirt and hair in a way that made me feel beautiful. Why, anything could happen.

Chances are your chances are awf'ly good . . . . *

His lanky form was but a foot away, and he smiled a smile just for me. "Dance with me, Abby?"

I nodded and was reaching for his outstretched hand.

Suddenly, I was falling . . . falling as if in slow motion into the Wangs' pool. The water was soothing.

Then I was drowning.

When I woke up, I was wetting the bed, and even the towel I had slept on hadn't absorbed everything. Shame flooded

*Chances Are. Lyrics by Al Stillman; music by Robert Allen. Copyright 1957 by Kitty-Ann Music Company and Charlie Deitcher Productions Inc.

through me like a white-hot river. What was the matter with me? Wet beds were for babies. What had I done to deserve this on top of everything else?

I tried not drinking anything after dinner, and increasingly, I lay awake at night, wanting to sleep to wipe away the trials of the day, needing to sleep because it took so much energy not to hear right, but reluctant to close my eyes lest I really fall into a slumber that might lead to another damp dawn. The warm trickle, the clammy thighs, the soaked bed linens despite the scratchy, twisted towel: where would it lead? Was I going to have to get some of those big disposable diapers old movie stars advertised on television?

"What are you doing?" my sister asked one morning. Everything about Paige was so perfect in contrast: her athletic prowess, her robust health, and the way she could do just about anything without straining. And, of course, she didn't wet the bed.

"What does it look like? Washing my sheets."

Did she suspect? How long would it be before she and everyone else caught on?

I'd die if my friends somehow guessed my secret. Why, it was so personal, so embarrassing, that I couldn't even tell Alison.

My mother figured out all the sheet washing. Concerned, she didn't have a clue as to why it was happening, but my doctor came up with the idea that it was only emotional. "Abby's going through a lot," the doctor said. Was that supposed to help? It only increased my disgrace and made me hate my stupid ears even more for, if the doctor was right, sabotaging my bladder.

If that wasn't bad enough, I was falling apart in other new ways. I had developed a puffy "moon" face from the latest medication prescribed to help my hearing. From the way I looked, my middle name should have been Dopey. Maybe worse, my emotions were all over the place. I started snapping at people for no reason, for instance, and I was so tired that I could hardly function.

"I just don't feel right," I told my parents.

"You have to give the steroid a longer try than this, Abby. The doctors at the clinic are convinced that it can save your hearing."

"Save my hearing? But I'm dying here."

"Don't be melodramatic." It was Dad, who had minimized every single feeling I had had, every single side effect from the by-then long string of drugs, every single everything from the time I had been sick. I knew that tone of voice, and I hated being considered overemotional. Couldn't they see what a shambles my life was? I guess not! He said what always got to me the most: "Don't you want to hear?"

Want to hear? How could he be so dumb? How could anyone, especially my own father, doubt that, when fear and panic sat on my shoulders like constant companions where my hearing was concerned? The ratio of good hearing days to bad days had lessened dramatically by then. There seemed to be nothing between the two extremes, either. I never knew what it would be when I woke up: a hearing day when I could actually talk to Alison on the phone and hear my teachers if I sat in front of the room, or a deaf day when I thought the lapses, the loneliness, the silence of it all would drive me insane. Who was I, anyway: a deaf girl, a hearing person, or someone caught in the middle who didn't fit in anywhere?

So, at the point I went to a famous clinic in another state, my fluctuating hearing was really screwing up my life and also panicking my parents. Even if it meant missing school and falling behind, I welcomed the chance to go to a world-renowned facility, sure that this place could help me if anywhere could.

There were the expected tests, scans, and probes. Of course the emphasis was upon my ears, but my vision, endocrine function, and you-name-it were checked. Looking back, what was ignored was how I felt. Although there was dialogue among the doctors and my parents, I might just as well not have been there.

What about my opportunity to ask questions, such as did they think I was going to become totally deaf, or what options were out there for me? When I conquered my shyness by speaking up, I was just dismissed by a professional smile or a "Not now, dear" from my parents. I was a teenager, fifteen by then, for heaven's sake, not seven, and I was hungry for information, needy of facts that might help me plot my life.

Since it was in the not knowing—the wondering and imagining all kinds of bleak scenarios—that I withered, I would have welcomed theories or educated opinions to help me deal with the morass into which I had fallen. How could it be that the doctors had stuck me with needles right and left, used sophisticated imagery to look at my brain, and invaded my most private parts without consideration for a bruised psyche? Why was I relegated to watching mouths flap when just maybe my input could have been as valuable for them as for me?

It was decided that I should try taking a steroid in an attempt to keep what little hearing I had left from degenerating even further. It would, they thought, as I learned later from my parents, reduce a swelling called cochlear hydrops and, perhaps, have other beneficial effects, so it was with a lot of hope in my heart, regardless of my dissatisfaction with their gross impersonality at the clinic, that I went home and began taking the big green horse capsules.

My hearing didn't improve or keep from worsening, but I did develop that puffy face, and I looked and felt half-asleep most of the time. I missed a lot of school after that because I was so tired, and in fact, often slept eighteen hours a day. I just couldn't keep my eyes open. The sum total, including the strange new snippiness, affected not only my schoolwork, but also my social life, and dulled my personal perceptions. The Japanese cherry blossoms might as well have been pumpkin-colored for all I noticed that spring. My parents didn't convey to me that they saw anything wrong with this. It was *The Clinic*, after all, that had put me on this course of medication, and wasn't anything okay if it was part of the noble battle to save my hearing?

I'd thought so, but now I was beginning to wonder.

Dad's voice again: "Don't you want to hear?"

What else could I do? Uneasily, I kept taking the steroid, scared that they were right and I would cut off the one thing that might keep me hearing, if only on my present hit-or-miss basis. Want to hear? I was the one living with all the gaps in conversations, all the distortion that turned sounds I had cherished into noise, the isolation, and the embarrassment of asking "What?" repeatedly or being center-stage when I despised it. Want to hear? Every ounce of my being wanted it.

How far do you go, though? The effort to save my hearing was spilling over into my life in ways that were depriving me of . . . well . . . *living*. Take the field trip with my history class to Seattle to see *Les Misérables* on stage, for example. In that lull just before the steroid storm, I felt pretty well. Going seemed doable. My hearing was bouncing all over the place, but I had relished the novel while recuperating from my illness, and besides, all my friends were going. My history teacher clinched it.

"You won't have trouble following," Mr. Ockwell said to me after class. "It's quite visual, and you know the story."

This particular production was supposed to be true to the book, so I signed up and was growing increasingly enthusiastic about going.

Then came the trip to the clinic and the downward spiral with the drug. Little by little, I began realizing that the play was out. I would be too sleepy. I might be too emotional, and, worst of all, what settled it was that probably I would wet the bed in the hotel room I was to share with at least two other students.

Couldn't I have anything—any fun—without something going wrong?

Mr. Ockwell didn't know where I was coming from, of course, when I tried to get out of it. He was one of my favorite teachers, not only because I liked history, but from the way he encouraged me to find my own way. He was sensitive without hovering, and he was helpful without offering suggestions that chipped away at my self-esteem or intelligence.

It wasn't surprising that he was nice now. "Oh, don't let a few days of missed school worry you, Abby. You have always been one of my best students. You deserve the trip."

I was in a limbo land, then, of knowing I couldn't go and yet not being able to say no so that it stuck.

As the weeks passed and the bedwetting and other symptoms got even worse, it dawned on me that the loss of control was one more side effect from the capsules that left such a bitter aftertaste.

This time, I begged my parents in no uncertain terms to let me stop. Were they blind or something not to see it for themselves? I just couldn't figure them out. Still convinced that the bedwetting was emotional and the other manifestations, worth it, they actually just pushed me to do more with Alison and my other friends, which only compounded my frustration. I was zombied out and embarrassed by my moon face, slowed speech, strange outbursts, etc., and terrified that word would get out that Abby Jensen wet her bed.

When Mr. Ockwell found out, thanks to Mom, I nearly died. I mean, Mr. Ockwell, of all people. How could I ever face him again?

"Mom! How could you?"

"I just told him the truth, Abby."

Livid, I wanted to vanish off the face of the earth. It was just so private a thing. Wasn't my plan just "to be sick" on the field trip day better? And now my history teacher knew I wet the bed!

Why was this even happening? It went deeper than a missed play. Why was I being tortured this way, being forced as I was to continue on a medication that was all but stopping my life?

I still don't know whether to laugh or cry at what finally made my parents see the light. Although I was again humiliated, it was probably fortunate that I wet the bed over spring break at my aunt's house in Astoria, because embarrassed themselves, my parents agreed at last that the side effects were outweighing the steroid's benefits. The proof was right there in the dry sheets. The other things, like the puffy face, lingered for a time, but to my enormous relief, the bedwetting stopped very fast once the drug was out of my system.

I'm glad I didn't know then that the steroid experience was only a precursor of the way my life was to become.

—CHAPTER SEVEN—

Increasingly, I found myself tiptoeing past my parents' room. I had gone from trying to help in any way I could—the pillow fluffing, the meal bringing, and the vain attempts to communicate—to just needing to stay away. I couldn't count the number of times I had entered the taupe and cream room, whose very color scheme had managed to change from serene to depressive, only to find my mother looking, still, like a broken doll. On one hand, I wanted to comfort her, but on the other, since she had rejected that, I felt like shaking her to reanimate her, making her Robin Jensen, *my mother*, again.

I had enough sense to realize that losing a child, no matter how old, no matter what the cause, must be the most excruciating loss in the world. My mother's retreat into herself might be the only way she could manage. It's just that regardless of how I tried to rationalize it, seeing her that way was heartrending, especially since I was hurting in my own right.

Just for a little conversation, I was glad when Dad approached me in the breakfast nook one morning. Did he look more Dad-like, or was it only wishful thinking? I got up and poured him a cup of coffee, black the way he liked it, and he took a sip of the steaming beverage. Lackluster these past weeks, at least he hadn't shut down to the extent that Mom had, yet he was still "gone," too, to somewhere private and painful, a place I was unable to penetrate. We danced verbally, never getting the beat right, never touching upon our innermost feelings about Abby's death. We talked, instead, about crazy things like the sprinkler system, which hardly mattered to either of us just then, so that our time together, what there was of it, was like an off-key melody.

When I sat down opposite him at the small round table, he was staring into his cup, perhaps seeing everything or noth-

ing at all, but still a galaxy away from me. *Come back!* I wanted
to scream.

Then a new emotion swept over me, as it had so often
lately. What was the matter with me, to feel flickers of anger at
my parents and at Abby herself for having thrust us into this
never-never land of sadness, regret . . . a welter of feelings that
twined around us like brambles? Was there no extrication?

Still, he was sitting there, living, breathing, and hadn't I
seen something a bit different in his expression just a moment
ago? Who knew? Maybe it would be better today. "Dad?"

He started. Then he spoke without preamble. "I'm
thinking about taking Mom somewhere." There was a decisive-
ness in his voice that I hadn't heard in weeks, and the weight in
my heart lessened for just an instant before I realized that
"somewhere" could mean anything.

Almost worse, with the pronouncement out, Dad had
stopped talking, and more than anything else, I didn't want my
father to leave me again. I had to keep him talking. I said, "I
know we have to do something. Dad, I've tried to make things
easier for her."

"I know, honey. I've been over this dozens of times, and
what I think she needs is a complete change of scenery. She
actually perked up slightly when I mentioned Greece."

"Greece?"

It was there in that moment that we seemed to turn a
communication corner onto old familiar ground, in the way his
look told me he had read my thoughts as he hadn't for some
time. When he spoke again, his voice actually sounded more
normal.

"Oh, you thought I might be talking about . . . ."

I nodded. "I think Greece sounds great. Mom used to
talk about how you went there before we were born."

"It's worth a try. You'll be all right?"

"As right as possible. I'm going to work part-time in the
tile and marble shop this summer." It was a far cry from the
office job in Chicago, but maybe in Delft tile and Italian marble

I would find my own escape and, perhaps, even some healing. "I'll be even more all right if when you return, Mom is better."

So, it had been decided.

The coming week actually brought me closer to Mom again. I was needed. In getting her clothes ready for the trip, even if we didn't say much, being in her room had a purpose, a comfort, that it hadn't since this ordeal had begun. One time I even turned from her closet to suggest that the turquoise sheath would be perfect for Greece's climate, and instead of being lost in the family album with those haunted eyes locked into the past, she was actually watching me. Her smile was as faint as the first hint of light at dawn, but there.

Something else happened that same week, although at the time I didn't know what to make of it. I had just returned from the dry cleaner's to hear raised voices coming from the living room. What in the world?

I didn't mean to eavesdrop, but I was trapped, cleaning in hand, in the foyer as a male voice I didn't recognize tore into someone I soon realized was my father: "You're way off base, Jensen."

"I wouldn't bet my last dollar on that, Cassidy," returned Dad, equally agitated.

Then, as I clutched the hangers, still rooted to the spot, a burly man about Dad's age and, I saw with surprise, Jay Cassidy, stormed past without seeming to see me.

I watched in amazement as Dad strode after them and slammed the door behind them. Then he turned around.

"Oh, Paige. You startled me!"

"What was that all about?"

"How much did you hear?"

For the two men to have been so angry, there had to have been a lot I hadn't heard. And Jay Cassidy? "Almost nothing, I guess."

"Good. It was just a stupid business matter. Let's let it drop. Here, let me take that. I see you have my slacks and navy blazer for the trip. Thanks."

Dad's obvious relief followed by his spate of words made me more curious than ever, but things had been going enough better at home that, especially with their trip coming up so soon, I didn't want to rock the boat by probing.

Maybe I should have.

When Mark Friedell called, I still had mixed feelings about our conversation at his house, but he quickly set me at ease, armed as he was with information and a plan of action that included my meeting with a couple of his friends who had been Abby's teachers.

"How did you know I was thinking about doing that?" I asked.

His smile was gentle. "I just guessed."

We had to wait to see the teachers, but caught up in my quest to learn what had happened to my sister, I started meeting Mark over lattes to talk about Abby. As time passed, we also exchanged information about ourselves, including what we liked and didn't like, and how we wanted to do our share to make the world a better place. Some of it was trivial. He enjoyed cross-country skiing and I didn't. I was a Chicago Bulls fan and he wasn't. But those differences were insignificant when put into the framework of emergent common values and, of course, our deep, shared interest in Abby.

Sometimes in the small talk there was solace, and other times the mundaneness of it all collided with the fact that my little sister was irrevocably gone. What difference did basketball make? Did it matter how many salmon could be caught legally this season? The world was revolving without my sister in it, and it seemed utterly impossible.

Some of my old high school friends had been supportive, but whereas most of them tiptoed around me or didn't understand my sudden reveries or mood swings, Mark seemed to, and in that space he gave me to be myself and grieve in my own time and way, I survived and grew to respect him in the process.

He didn't actually tell me much about Abby that I didn't already know. He confirmed her sensitivity, kindness, and other traits, and he lent perspective to what Alison had told me about, especially, Abby's final year. What meant so much to me was having someone with whom I didn't have to avoid saying Abby's name, someone I could talk to, someone with whom I could show my strange mixture of feelings. All along, I sensed that he had some deep emotions connected with my sister, but I trusted that they would come out in time, just as mine were with him.

One day we were eating Mexican food when the waiters' sombreros and a rush of loud music and clapping signaled someone's birthday. We were about finished with our own meal, and something about the party must have sent me into one of my little trances.

Mark's voice pulled me back. "Woolgathering?"

"Oh, I guess."

He looked at me searchingly. "I'm really dense. You were thinking about Abby, weren't you?"

I nodded and glanced toward the long table where the birthday celebrant was opening cards and gifts. "It's the birthday cards, I think. You wouldn't believe the sympathy cards that are still flooding in. This verse and that verse, as if words will make it better. Oh, that sounds awful of me, doesn't it? I do appreciate people's thoughtfulness, but I also feel like I'm drowning, Mark, in endless droplets of philosophy and religion that just don't seem to connect with what happened to Abby.

"And the personal notes are, at once, worse . . . and yet better, because they remind me, over and over in sometimes unexpected ways, of how special a person my sister was."

"I can see how that would be a double-edged sword. Are you thinking of something in particular?"

"I was thinking of the totality of them, but yes, one does come to mind. It was a letter from a woman that brought back a time when we already had a cat and a dog, and a little stray kitten that Abby immediately named Muffin wandered up to our porch and hung around. One more pet was out of the question, according to our parents, so we advertised it in *The Oregonian* as a winsome kitten."

Laughter bubbled at the memory, and Mark asked, "What tickled your funnybone just then?"

"Well, one woman who called to ask about the kitten wondered what she had to do to win some kittens." Mark smiled, but my laugh frittered away, foreign to me at a time when my heart felt so heavy. "Anyway, Abby and I were intent upon not just finding Muffin a home, but a good one. Finally, we heard just what we were looking for in a caller's voice. She didn't have much money, she said, so her seven-year-old daughter had to choose between a kitten and a Brownie uniform for her birthday.

"Let me guess. The kitten."

"Oh, yes. The girl wanted 'something soft and furry' to love. Abby, who was about nine at the time, just piped right up that maybe the girl could have both. Abby had treasured her own Brownie uniform because it had been mine, but she had moved up proudly to the green one. Still, she had vowed to let the old one 'forever and ever' have a special place in her closet. I think she might have, too, but she didn't have to think twice about sacrificing it to someone less fortunate.

"As Mom drove us over, I held Muffin, and Abby stroked the Troop 7 badge on her carefully folded uniform. I thought she might change her mind, but she didn't, and that other girl's eyes simply lit up to have two dreams come true on her birthday."

"That kind of giving sounds so like your sister. And you got a note from the girl?"

"From the mother, bringing back that memory and letting me know that Muffin is still hale, hearty, and loved, while the little brown dress was worn by her daughter and then passed on to another Brownie."

A shadow slid over Mark's expression.

"What is it, Mark?"

He shook his head and closed his eyes for a moment. I could tell that he had gone into himself, into an area of pain, and I was torn between needing to know what he was thinking and wanting to spare him.

When the waiter came just then with our check and Mark got caught up in paying it, I thought that I might never know what had veiled his thoughts so, but as we began walking home in the still-warm June air, he brought it up.

"I didn't mean to fade out on you in there."

"It's okay."

"It's hard to talk about, is all, not just from the standpoint of Abby but also in general terms."

"I would like to hear it if you want to tell me."

"Okay. It concerns . . . oh . . . what to me is a family tragedy, but the scope is vastly broader. I spoke to your sister of it because I saw something in her that made me think she might benefit from hearing my perceptions, although in light of what happened to her, I'm not positive I made the right decision. She was so sensitive."

The image of Abby in second grade sprang to mind: Abby feeling for a classmate named Wanda Kabosky, who had no mittens or warm winter coat. Abby had given Wanda her mittens and formulated a plan to help her by, with our mother's permission, giving Wanda a little-used ski jacket. The Kaboskys, too proud to accept even the kindness of a seven-year-old, had given the mittens back and closed the door on my sister, but that sensitivity to the needs of others had stayed with Abby through the Brownie uniform experience and all of her life.

I brushed away the memory and nodded, not sure what Mark was getting at. Family tragedy? Broad scope? I hoped he would fill me in without any prodding.

"Bear with me if this doesn't seem to relate at first to Abby," he said. We had stopped walking and sat on a low wall.

"Of course."

"Well, Mauthausen was one of the smaller of the World War II concentration camps, but no less horrible because of its size. My grandmother's family lived in that part of Austria, in Linz, and were caught up in Hitler's mad fantasy just because they were human and abhorred what was happening all over that part of Europe, including just down the river in the village of Mauthausen. Powerless to leave, they fought the Nazi atrocities in the only way they could, in the Resistance.

"Paige, they were discovered hiding a Jewish family of four in their attic."

I sucked in my breath as the memory of movies portraying just such acts of courage came to mind. "And they were . . . led away?"

He nodded somberly. "It was the end for them, for five people in my family, including my grandmother's little sister, not to mention the Jewish family."

"For being kind they were killed. Oh, Mark."

"I know. For reaching out a helping hand. It seems incredible. Impossible!"

"And your grandmother? Is this Madame Marek we are talking about? Was she in the camp?"

"Yes, it's she, but no, thankfully she wasn't in the camp. She was already an accomplished pianist when the war broke out, and by pure good fortune, she was out of the country, playing in England and staying with a cousin, when her family was taken away."

"How absolutely horrid for her."

"It happened over and over. It does hit closer to home when it's family."

I had the sudden vision of Mark's grandmother, always so patient with her pupils. She had a certain regal bearing, a grace, and now I thought that perhaps it was from carrying the mantle of survivorship. "I never knew. How could she not have been bitter?"

"It was something she talked about very seldom, but the memory was embedded in her soul and shone through in a particular kind of courage and kindness, which always amazed me, too. 'If Krisztina cannot be rancorous, then neither will I,' she explained. Krisztina was Grandmother's close girlhood friend who made it out of Mauthausen alive. She was due to be gassed with a group of women who had grown weak from the lack of food and unspeakable torture, but it was April 1945 and the camp was liberated before that happened. According to Grandmother, Krisztina, who had also lost her family, spoke time and again of the triumph of good over evil, in the continued nobility of myriad spirits tamped down by the worst kind of adversity.

"I had a chance to see the setting myself when I traveled to Austria."

"You went there?"

"I had to." He shook his head. "At first, I thought I had the wrong place, for I had expected a barren, bleak, salt mine type setting. Mauthausen, the village, though, sits along the Danube with a quaint prettiness much like any other in Austria, in beautiful countryside lush with trees, meadows, and gentle hills. It was up one of the hills, up above the village, that I found what is left of the camp."

He described the monuments along the ascent: among others, a plaque with hands reaching out for freedom, and a life-sized bronze tree defying wind, rain, and other onslaughts, with wreaths and commemorative bouquets everywhere.

"It was a touching prelude to a most stirring experience, but I won't bore you with the details."

"You aren't boring me."

He seemed pleased by my interest. "All right. At the crest of the hill, there was a stone wall and a rounded wooden door, oh, about the size of a double garage door and about twice as high, with smaller doors to either side. I parked the car in the graveled lot and stepped out to feel a rain as gentle as soft, spent tears. It's when I looked at the looming portal to nowhere that I was hit by probably the most profound feeling I have ever had, Paige, a visceral punch that simply crumpled something inside me. Seeming to see the thousands upon thousands of people with luggage marching through, most never to return, I had such a distinct feeling of their spirits all around me that for a moment the oxygen might as well have been sucked from the air I was breathing. I broke down and sobbed, and I couldn't stop for just the longest time."

By the way his voice quavered, he was on the verge of weeping now, and something in me—some significant part of my soul—seemed to merge just then with his as I imagined the door and the multitudes caught up in a madman's dream.

He shifted his position and told me about the preservation of some of the barracks-like "dorms" inside the wall, the hospital where terrible experiments had been conducted, and the most horrifying building of them all, the death house with its concrete steps leading down to a room where people were shot or unsuspectingly herded into another chamber with showers through which deadly Zyklon B gas was piped in to unrelentlessly snuff out their lives behind locked steel doors. The cavernous room where bodies were temporarily warehoused and the ovens were soul-searing postscripts.

"It is odd, though," Mark continued, "that for me the worst came in the museum. That's where the mass of Holocaust victims became individual human beings: grandmothers once redolent of torte, fathers with stories to tell, teachers and tradespeople, and children ripped from their mothers' arms. There were descriptions of Mauthausen and the different major camps, such as Auschwitz and Dachau, and a few artifacts. The lists of the condemned were methodical, precise, and chilling: so many men and women killed in a particular month, so many children, a handful of homosexuals, a group of others deemed inferior, all with individualities burned away, at least in the minds of their captors, in a mad blaze of intolerance. Pictures that will haunt me forever include one of a small mountain of suitcases once carried by people who may have felt they were only being relocated, and then another of piles of jewelry stripped from them as they entered the camp."

And piles of corpses, I knew. I had seen archival footage on television, but to hear a firsthand account of such a place, even sanitized as it was when Mark had seen it, made it all the more real. "My God!"

"But the worst," he went on so softly that I had to strain

to hear, "the worst was the dress."

"The dress?"

"It was a real dress, a little brown wool one, and it could have, in my way of thinking, fit my grandmother's eight-year-old sister, Elisabeth."

"The one who never returned?"

He nodded.

"It had a . . . an *X* painted across the top . . . a large, unmistakable *X* . . . ."

His words faltered completely then, and as he rose, his head dropped into his hands as a single sob erupted gasplike from the depth of him. I stood and put my arms around him, feeling his body quiver against mine in a grief that I knew was unending.

An *X* on a child's dress: just a little girl, maybe even Elisabeth, who had been consigned to death because of her heritage, her disability, or whatever dark reason had propelled her murderers to decree that this human being should become cordwood, ashes . . . no more.

Still close to Mark, I hadn't realized that I was crying until I felt his hand brush away my tears. Our eyes met and locked in shared feeling. Then our lips came together, and his kiss was infinitely tender.

That life-affirming moment in the midst of such dark images both soothed and startled me. When we broke apart, surprised at what had happened, we looked away from each other, perhaps embarrassed, certainly at a loss for words just then. Just which one of us had initiated it, I wasn't even sure. I only knew that it had been healing, and more.

When I finally looked at Mark again, not sure what I would find, relief washed over me as I saw reflected in his faint smile that he felt the same way. No words, after all, needed to be said right then. I liked the way when he spoke again, it was simply a continuation of our conversation.

"Paige, I shared some of this with Abby, especially the part about Krisztina, my grandmother's friend, and the way they tried to extract every last drop of humanity, only to have her defy them, and prevail, by spiritually transcending her surroundings and abject abuse. Her freedom of attitude both then and after her liberation inspires me, and it was this that I tried to convey to your sister."

I wasn't sure I got the connection, and Mark must have sensed it.

"The more I talked to Abby, the more I realized that although the circumstances are vastly different—and I'm not downplaying the enormity of the Holocaust—there are some parallels. Abby didn't ask to get sick and have her life turned upside-down. She didn't ask or deserve to be misunderstood, labeled, led along, and occasionally belittled. Her illness was one thing, but the way people sometimes treated her, and the way I saw something in her that suggested draining hope and fight, reminded me of the oppression I had heard about from *Mutti*, my grandmother."

"But, Mark, I'm not sure I understand. Abby had all kinds of options. Krisztina and the other people in Mauthausen didn't."

"Didn't they? That's what I was trying to say. To be sure, they couldn't walk out through the big door to freedom or usually avoid being starved, persecuted, or gassed. No way am I trying to lessen their plight. But while they lived, Paige, *while they lived*, most had the option to find spiritual freedom. They could give in or they could draw upon love and all the other human traits we hold dear as they struggled to survive. Each day became a triumph, according to Krisztina. Each flicker of hope. Each small act of defiance. Each kindness to or from another prisoner. Humanity could, and did, become their salvation, even if in the end their bodies perished. Now, that might seem like a paltry thing, if in the end they died anyway, but if you really think about it, that kind of transcendence, that kind of freedom and the courage to exercise it well, is the very essence of our being."

"And you wanted Abby to find this freedom and exert it."

"Oh, yes!"

"How did she react?"

"She was sobered by the thought of Mauthausen, of course. I left out the part about the dress and some of the other details. Abby died so soon after our conversation that I simply don't know if she got the connection I was trying to make: overcoming odds on a day-to-day basis and prevailing."

"I'm sure you inspired her," I said.

"Did I? I hope so."

"Then what's wrong?" There it was again, that shadow that I had first seen at his house after the funeral, and I knew it had to do with something more than the horrors of Mauthausen. I hoped he wouldn't clam up now, and he didn't.

"I didn't mean to minimize the trials of Abby's life by mentioning the concentration camp. The suffering there was without comparison, on a level we can only imagine; even then, I'm sure that we can't fully comprehend something that extreme unless we have lived it. Because it's so profound, I'm worried that I inadvertently made Abby feel diminished and somehow lacking in her coping skills. I could just kick myself for neglecting to tell her that suffering is relative."

"Relative? Yes, I guess it is," I agreed, wondering at the same time to what extent my sister had suffered. Obviously, since she had taken her own life, it had seemed great to her. *Seemed* was probably the operative word, I thought with a sigh, and maybe the image of Mauthausen had only exacerbated Abby's feelings, but she was gone and Mark was so alive, so unsure of himself in this matter. I could see him wondering what had gone through my sister's mind, see blame in his eyes, and I touched his arm gently as I said, "I'm sure you conveyed the positive legacy of that terrible time."

"How can you be?"

"I just am. You've proven your kindness to me in the way you tried to help Abby and in your deep feelings for what happened at Mauthausen. Mark, I've been down that road a dozen times—no, more than that—these past weeks: 'What if I'd done this for Abby; what if I had said that?' and it's futile. In many ways, I didn't know my sister anymore, and for that I feel guilty, but I knew her well enough to believe that she would have listened well and completely; she would have picked up on your meaning. You were a good influence in her life."

"Thanks." His brief smile melted away. "You weren't sure of that when you came to my house, were you?"

I looked away, ashamed of my one-time suspicion that he might have played a negative role in her life. "I'm sorry."

"It's all right. I read somewhere that doubting, and sharing that feeling, can ultimately be a bridge to trust."

"I hope so."

Already he was learning to read me. "What?" he asked.

"Oh, I don't know. I keep coming back to the same thing. It's just that no matter how I try to rationalize it, no matter what the facts seem to indicate, I still can't believe Abby committed suicide. Suicide, Mark! She was so against it. What happened to make her violate her principles? What pushed her over the edge?"

"I don't know, except that we do all have a breaking point."

The more I thought about that, the more convinced I was that deafness had been Abby's.

⊸Chapter Eight⊱

Abby　My life actually improved before it got worse. Once the effects of the steroid started wearing off, it was as if a light went back on. My thoughts came back into sharper focus, I looked better, and I stayed awake longer hours.

Maybe it was part of adapting, especially in the wake of the steroid fiasco, but my daily routine became a series of "at least's." My hearing wasn't good, but at least I felt physically more like my old self again. I slept over at Alison's with two other friends, and although I felt left out when I didn't get everything they said, especially once the lights were off, at least I didn't wet my sleeping bag. I saw Jay Cassidy on the stairs at school and hoped he would smile at me, but if he didn't, at least I knew my face was no longer a big puffy moon. And although I missed a lot in the classroom, at least I was going to school regularly again. It was just about the smoothest sailing I had had since I was sick.

That isn't to say the reality of not hearing right wasn't sometimes crushing. It never really got any less terrible, because when you have lost such an important sense, you just always have to go the extra mile to get what other people take for granted.

My hearing loss, though, didn't feel quite as claustrophobic with passing time. I was learning, for instance, to use my eyes as I never had before, instead of just straining, sometimes so futilely, to hear. Little by little, where there had been empty spots in sentences, there were words, thoughts, and meaning. I figured out that certain sounds look exactly alike on the lips, such as with *mat*, *bat*, and *pat*, and once I held language keys like that, what I didn't hear wasn't necessarily lost in space. It truly amazed me the way my brain was like a computer, working in split-seconds to change one unclear word to another if what I thought I saw didn't make sense. It might look like "The *mat* flew out of the cave," but since that didn't make any sense, my mind would rapidly substitute the word *bat*, which made all kinds of sense. It wasn't easy and sometimes I missed connections—it certainly didn't by a long shot approximate hearing—but it effectively showed me that I wasn't as cut off as I had at first thought I was.

That, and realizing that there was nothing wrong with asking for help, allowed me to apply myself in new ways in school. Oh, I was still shy, and sometimes it mortified me to be singled out, but more often than before, I was able to delineate both my strengths and limitations. "I would like to try it," I might say if a teacher thought I couldn't do something. "Would I be able to substitute a paper for the oral portion?" I would suggest if I knew my hearing would make me bomb out in a certain situation. Most times, the teachers were receptive and even grateful for my input.

I also found somebody in most of my classes who was willing to take notes for me, which freed me from worrying about missing essential material. Notetaking also rejoined me with the class by letting me in on the jokes, an aside from the back of the room, and the teachers' anecdotes that went a long way toward fleshing out basic information. Except with one teacher who was blind enough to reprimand my notetaker and me for "writing notes" in class, it went well.

I was getting by.

Just when everything was finally going better, my parents decided to make one last-ditch effort to make me hear better. About all that was left after our unhappy trail of drugs was electrical amplification, which Dad had balked at, perhaps because he thought medication could work wonders. Since I was fed up with all the side effects, luckily for me we had exhausted the chemical possibilities. Then Dad did an about-face.

I had mixed feelings about the idea of a hearing aid. Even with my new visual skills, I was left out enough on the bad hearing days that I wanted the few remaining better ones to happen all the time. If a hearing aid could do that, so be it, I guessed.

On the other hand, even though I knew people of all ages wore them, I associated them with senior citizens. Good grief! I was only fifteen. I didn't want to feel like an instant old person or to call even more negative attention to myself because it showed. I cringed to think people might look at me and think, "Oh, there goes THE HEARING AID."

Still, almost anything was better than struggling so hard to understand or having one more side effect, so when I was finally retested and the right aid chosen for me, I was relieved to find that it fit neatly behind my good ear. It was actually with an open mind that I started wearing it.

I had problems from the outset. I hadn't expected it to be perfect, and I had even been warned that it would take some time to get used to it, but it hurled me into a world of such confusion, distortion, distraction, and total exasperation that it was as if a dark curtain had been drawn back over my life.

Where I had once felt trapped by the silence, I was now ensnared by continuous noise that actually hindered my effort to understand. The electronically induced cacophony not only ruined my ability to concentrate upon newly discovered visual speech clues, but exaggerated sounds that once had had meaning into earsplitting hisses and pops and rumbles. The word *baseball*, which I might have distinguished on a speaker's lips before, now blasted through the hearing aid as *aaay-aaah*, which sounded for all the world to me like a donkey's bray. In fact, there was an entire animal farm of sounds that ranged from goose honks to moos. Other tones were obviously lost in that void even the hearing aid couldn't fill with sound, and I had a headache most of the time from listening so hard and wincing at too-loud sounds so that I could, hopefully, pick up the softer ones like little crumbs.

The assault happened everywhere I wore the hearing aid. At home, it channeled in inconsequential toilet flushes, the bark of the neighbor's pesky dog, and even the distant wail of a train's horn, but when it came to understanding speech, forget it. My parents might suddenly just as well have been speaking an alien language.

It was also a social disaster. Being somewhere like Sage's for a hamburger was where I wanted to be. Wasn't it where all my friends hung out? The hearing aid, though, turned being there into a slow torture as it electronically bombarded me with piped-in music, cackles, and rising voices, not to mention the exaggerated clinks of glassware, chair scrapes, and the occasional persistent cry of a fussy baby.

I was there on a Friday evening with four friends when the noise level was so high that I had to turn off the hearing aid or go bonkers. I was getting by because Alison remembered to include me now and then. Kaitlyn Forney never even looked my way. Remembering the way she liked to talk about people, I guessed I wasn't missing much, and heaven knew the silence was preferable to the hearing aid assault.

I ate some fries, salting them the way I liked.

All of a sudden, Kaitlyn's almost frantic waving got my attention. Oh, great! She had finally decided to include me just at one of those moments I had stopped watching so intently. Couldn't she have waited ten seconds until I looked up again?

I think she said something like, "Abby, are you there?" Whatever her exact words were, the irritation scarring her face brought any number of rejoinders to mind, like, *What do you see? Of course I'm here.*

I said, "Oh, what?"

I forced myself to smile as she took another bite of burger. Then she said something with her mouth full. Was I going to have to ask her to repeat . . . again?

Alison helped me out. "She said she thought you could hear with your hearing aid on," I read on her lips.

Kaitlyn chewed and swallowed and then looked at me with the most awful challenge in her expression that suggested what a stupid, royal pain I was.

"It's not on," I said, ready to explain why I turned it off sometimes. For her, I'd even add how maybe, just maybe, I could read her lips if she'd even bother to try. My explanation died on my lips as she just rolled her eyes.

So, I learned fast that people expected a hearing aid to be as effective as a pair of glasses or contacts, and didn't understand when it wasn't. I had a new left-out feeling that merely crippled my social life instead of augmenting it.

"You have to give the hearing aid a good try," everyone from my parents to audiologists to my doctor insisted, and I did, but time and again, I had to rip it off to stay sane.

If it was bad at home or with friends, it was excruciating in school because what I missed was more glaring. Where the teachers were concerned, it picked up their voices willy-nilly, with an abundance of new, strange sounds that blanked out words I had been getting without the hearing aid. Male voices tended to rumble or drone, while the higher-pitched female ones often got lost or pierced almost hurtfully.

What probably was a good discussion became a mind-boggling mélange: rumble . . . cough . . . paper crinkles . . . scrapes. When one morning Jerome Pelter's tap-tap-tap of a pencil behind me came through in small explosions interfering with the reception of my teacher's low drone, I thought, *I can't stand it, I can't stand it . . . .* Where was comprehension? I *was* giving it a good try, but how were these distractions supposed to help me understand my teachers and the other students? Was it really better to hear these things than have them lost in silence, as they had been before?

I returned from school daily so frustrated, so devoid of feeling I had learned anything, and usually with my head splitting, that my room, and taking off the aid, was a pleasant sanctuary of silence. Again, I slept long hours, needing to recharge myself from the new ordeal.

My parents seemed understanding when I told them how awful it was. We tried another model. And then another. The results were similar, and I was getting behind in my home-work. I was also feeling increasingly alone.

It was at this point, with what I considered the failure of

the hearing aid, that something clicked: Maybe we had done all we could and what I heard without the aid was as good as it was ever going to get. There are simply no words to describe the impact of that moment, and yet I wonder if in the back of my mind, I hadn't slowly been coming to realize that our efforts to restore my hearing were doomed.

As dark and unwelcome as the feeling was, I knew I had to let go. I couldn't go through life, could I, chasing a will-o'-the wisp?

"Maybe this is just the way it's going to be," I said to my parents more than once about my hearing, and if I tried to tell them I thought that maybe they were dreaming a dream beyond our control to realize, they just got angry or turned silent. I think sometimes they actually still thought I didn't want to hear! Every fiber of my being wanted to, but I had needs beyond that. In their quest to keep my hearing as normal as possible, and especially in such blatant emphasis upon it, they were denying that I was still me, still a person with feelings that went far beyond my hearing.

I didn't want to be yanked out of school anymore for doctors' appointments. I felt doubly self-conscious if I had been at some clinic for days at a time, because returning to school brought the inevitable "Where have you been's" and meant lots of catching up, which was no mean feat at those times when I had been feeling terrible from some side effect. Why couldn't I sit down and talk about anything with my parents other than their self-appointed mission? Didn't Mom see that I had a figure, I liked boys, and might want a little advice? Didn't Dad ever stop to consider that I might still be interested in practice-casting in the yard? I tried to tell them my needs, tried to get them to hear, but they let me know repeatedly that anything not directly related to my hearing, and to some extent my grades, wasn't "relevant."

It got especially bad when I realized that my mother still prayed every night for my hearing to return to normal. She had told me her exact prayer at one time, and I was touched, especially since I wanted it to be answered as fervently as she did, but when she kept on asking as time passed and my hearing diminished, I became irritated and then exasperated. Was she really even praying for me at this point? Did she think I had to hear to be happy and whole? Worse, were my parents going to start loving me less if I didn't hear better? To what extent in their eyes was my hearing a measure of my success? And what, heaven forbid, would happen if it left altogether?

It was upsetting enough thinking about that without worrying about their reactions. And I worried a lot. I was afraid of screwing up in school, afraid I would lose more friends or not make new ones, and I was terrified most of all of also going blind. What would I do then? I also worried about the future, like walking down the aisle at my wedding and keeping time to music I couldn't hear, or wondering how if I had a child and couldn't hear, I could answer the zillions of little questions a preschooler asks her mother. What about a career? What was out there for someone like me? What about being loved? No one addressed those thoughts, even if I tried to bring them up. For everyone else, it seemed that my life had turned into the mere mechanics of hearing.

And what I wanted most was not so much to hear as to be heard.

Even though I was smothering in a pall of grating gibberish and noise, I kept on with the hearing aid.

"Give it a longer try," my parents insisted in their best no-nonsense mode.

"You are fighting it," one audiologist decided.

"You will lose the rest of your hearing if you don't keep the nerve stimulated," a doctor informed me, which certainly scared me into wearing it.

And I did try, but the jumbled sound wasn't getting any better, and my headaches were becoming worse and more frequent. To survive, I turned the stupid thing off a lot in school and with my friends. As for my parents, it was as if I didn't know them anymore. It's odd, too, since in some ways, they were the nicest people I had ever known. *Were* is the key word, I suppose. I don't know what happened or exactly when it did. It's just that they had become one of the biggest frustrations since my illness, shutting me out of decision making, for instance, as well as incessantly focusing upon my hearing at the expense of me as a whole person. *I'm here; I'm me!* my inner voice cried. It wasn't that I didn't appreciate their concern and drive to save my hearing, but how could I not also despise it for the way it began to rob me of myself?

A case in point is the piano. I had returned from school, tired from a long day of mini-struggles that didn't seem so small at the time, to find our baby grand piano gone. It had taken up a large corner of our living room, and it was just obviously missing.

I had a weird feeling.

"Is the piano out for some kind of repair?" I asked Mom, realizing that there was more to it. People didn't often send baby grands out for anything, except, I guessed, for refinishing. That must be it.

That piano meant the world to me. My earliest memory, in fact, is of sitting beneath it with Mom playing popular tunes. She hit any number of clunkers, but she loved what she was doing, and maybe that's partly why I took to it so easily and completely. To complement that, my father, although he didn't play, had always been a music buff. He gravitated toward Dixieland jazz and knew of musicians like Wingy Manone and the Dukes of Dixieland, but he also had an extensive classical music collection of CDs and prized old records that he played, especially, on Sunday afternoons while he caught up on medical journals or just rested. So, music surrounded me from my earliest and best recollections.

By the time I was four, as the story goes, I was pecking out melodies of my own, and when I was five, according to Mom, she walked up to the piano one day and asked what I was playing.

"'Concerto to the Balloons,'" I said, probably having

given my piece the most delightful title I could think of.

"It sounds nice. Where did you hear it?"

"On TV. A man was waving a stick, and they were playing it. It's pretty."

"It certainly is."

When Dad heard me play, he informed me that it was Tschaikovsky's famous *Concerto No. 1 in B-flat Minor.*

Fixated upon my mental image, I insisted that we call it "Concerto to the Balloons."

"You may certainly do that," Dad assured me. Then he and Mom put their heads together.

"Abby," Mom asked, "would you like to learn to play all the notes to 'Concerto to the Balloons' and other pieces?"

My nod became my own decision to start piano lessons, which also began my relationship with Georgia Marek, a retired concert pianist under whose tutelage I flourished to the extent that competitions and even a career as a concert pianist were mentioned as the years passed. My parents never pushed it. I liked to practice, savored learning new pieces, and as I developed my skill, music was both a friend and the essence of my soul, speaking just to me and out to others in ways I couldn't because of my shyness.

In the living room, back in the present, I looked again at the void where the piano had been and then back to Mom, who walked closer and enunciated so clearly that there was no doubt about what she said.

The words were devastatingly simple. "We sold it."

"You . . . sold it?" Even though I had seen her words, I had the hearing aid off and must have misread them.

She said something else. What lipreading skills I had been mastering had suffered with the intrusion of the hearing aid's noise, and now my creeping fear got in the way.

"What?"

"Things are different now."

Different now? She was telling me? "Yeah, I'm almost deaf, but you know I still like to play. Mom, how could you? It was my piano!"

"Do you, Abby? Do you really still like to play? It didn't look that way when I saw you crying at the keyboard."

"So, you just sold it without even talking to me about it first?"

"We did it for your own good, honey. You need to channel your energy into more reasonable activities."

I was incredulous. "Reasonable?"

I'll always wonder why I didn't rant and rave. A part of me detached itself from my body and raced to the wall and pounded it down to chunks of wallboard and paint flecks. Why didn't I tell her that they had sold a piece of my soul by taking away my music? Why was I like that? Did I know how futile it would have been?

I had tried speaking up about my hearing, but like the ocean tide, my parents had crested over me so many times that I was losing my voice. And how could selling the piano be in my best interest? Sure, maybe I would never play in front of a large audience, as we had thought I might someday, but I was still playing, if only sporadically because so much was going on. Didn't that count for something?

What about how I felt about playing? At least in playing with my fingers, even if I didn't hear the notes perfectly, and even if I turned my hearing aid off to still the magnified discordant sound it produced, I heard in my memory the old way as I found the appropriate notes and kept all kinds of compositions alive.

Oh, sure, I had cried in front of the keyboard. What did she expect? From the time I had awakened from the coma, music had never sounded right, so how could I not miss the wonderful blending of notes? But I remembered that time she had caught me crying at the piano. I remembered it, all right. If she had bothered to ask me, to consider my feelings, she would have found out that my tears that day were products of the shattering experience of hearing my lovely piano blare through the hearing aid, grotesque beyond imagination, for the very first time.

The response she had witnessed that day had been to the hearing aid, not the piano. Why, then, was it the piano that had to go? Hearing aid turned off, I had played again, but had she seen the relief? Had she ever stopped to think that music spoke to my vital inner core?

That piano was a part of me!

"Reasonable," I said again as I stared at the vacant spot where it had been. "Yeah, the only 'reasonable activities' are part of your self-appointed battle to save my hearing.

"What about saving me?"

—Chapter Nine—

When I pressed the bell, a light flashed rhythmically through the doorside window.

"I'm Melissa," an auburn-haired woman of about fifty introduced herself as she ushered me into a modern townhouse whose interior had an unexpected Old World flavor.

Just talk normally, but not too fast, and be sure to look at me. And don't swish your hands, Abby had schooled. *That's distracting.*

"I'm Paige. Thank you for seeing me," I enunciated carefully without exaggerating. Melissa Black was, according to her husband, a speechreader, and I was thankful for Abby's little lesson.

Now, as Melissa led me through a living room rife with chintzes, beautiful woods, and porcelain plates used decoratively, it was as if Abby herself might have decorated it, and I faltered for just a moment as it hit me that I was here, talking to a stranger, trying to find Abby, who would never be able to appreciate the Britishness of the home.

It was almost a relief to pass through the Abbyesque room, onto a wooden deck with wrought-iron furniture made inviting with plump green-and-white striped cushions and flowers in pots and hanging baskets. A Siamese cat lay curled into a ball in a splash of sunshine on one chair and brought my focus back to the woman I had come to see.

We sat down, facing each other. "Justin filled me in. I'm so sorry for your loss, Paige, and I'll do everything I can to give you as clear a picture as possible of what it's like to be deafened as a teenager."

"Thank you. Your husband said you were about the same age as Abby when you lost your hearing."

She poured two tall glasses of tea from a frosty pitcher, and the clink of ice momentarily brought the cat to life. It looked at us and yawned before resuming its slumber.

"That's Mariko," Melissa informed me as she handed me a glass. "Yes, and I even had the same illness, but remember that I'm me and Abby was Abby. There may be some universals to losing one's hearing at that age, but take care not to assume that your sister felt all my feelings or had the same things happen to her that did to me."

"That seems fair."

Melissa sighed. "Where do I begin? I was a regular little girl, into 1950s things, with dreams of becoming a nurse, a bride, and a mother. I went swimming at a lake with friends a lot that summer I was fourteen, and I guess that's where I contracted meningitis. I was in a coma for several days, and when I woke up, my hearing was down, but it didn't really dawn on me until later, when I started feeling stronger, that my hearing loss was going to be permanent. It was so profound a realization that I have blotted out many of the feelings—feelings that were probably still fresh for Abby."

It sounded so grim. I didn't want to pry, but I had to know. "Do you mind if I ask what kinds of feelings?"

"Of course I don't, but it's difficult to put some things into words because they are so complex, pervasive, and, sometimes, hurtful. There was a separation from the friends who didn't understand what was happening to me or change their pace a little to include me, and isolation when I sat down at the dinner table at big family gatherings and most of my relatives seemed to forget that I was there. Even when I was ostensibly included, I missed things. People weren't looking directly at me, they had droopy mustaches or thin lips that impeded lipreading, or I hadn't followed the conversational ball to the next speaker in time to see what I needed to. Naturally, I filled in the words I missed as best I could—lipreading is a guessing game almost as much as it is a skill—but some things don't translate easily, such as 'Mary Ellen broke up with John and went out with _____ last night.' It sounds silly now, but when you're fourteen or fifteen, that kind of lapse is crucial, believe me."

I smiled.

"Of course, it meant missing important things, too: 'The test will include material on chapters twelve through ____teen.' I would ask for clarification for something like that, but basically all the *What's* got tiring, and sometimes when you are young, you just don't want to call attention to yourself by asking people to repeat on a regular basis. People's attitudes certainly shape this reluctance: a bored look at having to explain or repeat, exasperation at having one's narrative interrupted by a *what*, or the implication that you are a dud at lipreading. No one likes to feel like a nuisance or a dunce."

When she paused to take a sip of iced tea, I did too, and I felt like I was ingesting the images of how difficult it had been for her at the same time I drank. How many times had I been irritated as I repeated for Abby, and I was her own sister! I listened carefully as Melissa resumed speaking.

"I hated waking up in the morning sometimes to face all over again that my life was different and that it was such a struggle to do what I had taken for granted. It was awakening to another day of *what*-ing and missing my old familiar world, some days more than others. Oh, the gaps were hurtful, Paige, and some couldn't be filled in by even the most patient repetition. I was missing things like the Top Forty the kids were talking about and I couldn't hear right. I still had some hearing then, but some of the most popular singers and groups sounded like crickets chirping instead of musicians. A song called, I think, *Hey, Little Devil* was 'Aay, Dibble Dibble' to me. The words were gibberish and the melody, tinny before music became nothing at all."

"Do you hear anything at all now?"

"Not a glimmer. But even back when I still had some, there were missed phone calls, the lifeline of any teenaged girl. I longed for birdsong, the crunch of October leaves underfoot, the sound of raindrops on the roof, and the choirs in church. The list could go on and on, and I'm sure Abby's was as endless as mine, for when you have heard, the absence of sound leaves an aching void, especially when one is new to it and caught in the throes of change."

Melissa's words cut through me. I knew music must have headed Abby's list, as well as the uninterrupted flow of conversation, but what else? I didn't know, and that lack of knowledge stung.

"What are you thinking?" Melissa asked.

"That I don't know what Abby's list was."

"I'm sorry. I didn't get that."

The lapse in my knowledge about my sister had brought such a rush of emotion that I had forgotten to look at Melissa, so I repeated and added, "I can figure out the major ones but not the little things that added up and probably hurt her every single day."

"It's not necessarily something one shares. Not only is something like that difficult to put into words, but it can unintentionally invite pity."

But shouldn't I have guessed? Had I known my sister at all after her illness, known what had struck to the core of her? Then again, that's why I was here. If I let my guilt and regret consume me, I would never gain new perspectives that might shed light onto the dark corners of my mind and ultimately let me see Abby.

"I guess so," I said. "Melissa, what was school like for you? Abby's grades were fine, but I'm wondering now if she wasn't carrying those hurts around and hiding some of her experiences to spare us, or whatever."

"Simply because there were so many of them, she probably was. School is a tricky setting, educationally and emotionally, for a person who doesn't hear normally. It's so complex that I don't know where to start. I had some other physical problems following my illness, so in addition to the expected verbal gaps in my comprehension of teachers and discussions, my having been sick permeated my high school days in ways that probably nobody, including I, could have foreseen, such as when I was initiated into Latin Club."

"You were able to take Latin?"

For a moment, Melissa looked stern. Then she smiled. "I lost my hearing, not my intelligence. Latin isn't a snap, but it was mainly mastering declensions: *amo, amas, amat,* etc., and learning irregular verbs and vocabulary. There were oodles of written exercises, as opposed to the living languages which require a balance of oral work, so in some ways it was perfect for me."

"Tell me about the initiation."

"It doesn't relate directly to deafness."

"That's okay. You've piqued my interest."

She smiled again. "Well, dressed as Roman slaves, we inductees had to take turns standing blindfolded on a chair, where we were inspected by prospective owners and eventually 'bought' by an older club member, who owned his or her slave for the next day at school. At school, we had to wear our togas and signs proclaiming us as slaves—*Sum serva Diane,* for instance—and our masters gave us chores that ranged from carrying their books to tying their shoelaces and even scratching their backs.

"Anyway, when it was my turn, I was put onto the chair and twirled around. I didn't know beforehand what the effect would be, but with my eyes covered and impaired balance on top of it, I just keeled right over and probably would have been hurt if someone hadn't caught me. It doesn't sound so bad now, but at the time, when I was fifteen or so, it was humiliating, especially when someone piped up that I was feeble. It was such negative attention at a time that should have been a lot of fun. A feeble slave? Who would buy me? I was mortified, Paige, and realized that I must have been out of my mind to be joining the club. Thanks to the illness, I could hardly walk with my own books, let alone act as a slave carrying someone else's. It's just that I liked Latin and wanted so badly to be normal and fit in."

She took another, longer swig of tea.

"Well, don't keep me hanging. Did someone buy you?"

"Yes, thank heavens. Diane was a year ahead of me in school, a former neighbor. The ancient Romans would have rolled over at her purchase and the gentle tasks she gave her slave, but I was enormously grateful for her compassion. I was lucky."

"Lucky? Well, I'm glad it worked out, but it still sounds awful."

"It was in many ways, but downers like that in my life were balanced by acts of kindness such as Diane's, my true friend Julie's steadfastness, the teachers who listened, and a special boy whose very face made my heart sing, even though he never knew I was head-over-heels in love with him."

I smiled, remembering the feeling. "I think it was balanced for Abby, too. I hope so. She had a best friend, Alison, who remained constant, some good teachers, and this guy she was crazy about, although I don't really understand . . . . "

When I paused, wondering again why Abby hadn't gone out with Jay, Melissa asked, "Understand what?"

"It's strange. Not long before she died, this guy finally asked Abby out, and she turned him down. I just don't get it. She had hoped for that for just the longest time."

"And she never said why?"

"No, and I guess we'll never know."

"Maybe not, but to lend a little perspective, I can remember turning a guy down because I thought I'd bomb out at a movie by not being able to discuss the dialogue intelligently afterwards or hear his whisper during the show. This guy of Abby's might have asked her to a dance where she thought she wouldn't be able to follow him well enough without hearing the music normally. There are so many scenarios."

For a moment, I felt shell-shocked. *Scenarios?* At Abby's age, I had worried about my hair, a zit, or what to wear on a date, while Abby must have had an extra set of variables and emergent problems connected to her deafness that went far beyond what I had imagined. Even after the way Abby had died, it just really hit me then: the fears, the worries, the complexity of the changes brought on by her illness. Had anyone called my sister feeble or worse? What situations had she been cast into, and how many

Dianes had been there to bail her out?

I didn't know, and it hurt beyond measure. My sister's absence engulfed me once again.

"I'll be right back," Melissa said, and when she returned, she handed me a tissue. I had been crying without even realizing it.

"I'm sorry," I said.

"No need to apologize. Paige, although it's an entirely different situation, I lost my father about six months ago. It wasn't tragic, as your sister's death certainly is, because he had lived a long full life, but I know how powerful memories are and how all kinds of thoughts glide in and out, unbidden."

"I'm sorry about your father."

"Thanks. The breeze is one of those things that now makes me think of him."

"The breeze? How so?"

"'I am a thousand winds that blow; I am the diamond glints on snow'—just a fragment from a poem, but I feel that my father is now those things, and when the wind touches me, I think of him and am comforted.

"I can't imagine what it must be like to lose a sister so young. I've had a hard enough time dealing with the empty spot left by my father's passing. He was just such a large presence. All I can say is how sorry I am and offer the small comfort that time does heal even the deepest wounds."

Her words might have been trite, but weren't because they came from her heart and also made me remember why I was there: to glean information, perspective, and understanding. I nodded, somehow ready to continue our discussion.

"You mentioned the Latin Club initiation. What was school like for you on the whole? What makes a good teacher for a deaf student?"

"Wow. Justin would like that latter question. I can't speak for anyone but myself, and keep in mind that I was in high school before mainstreaming and special ed classes for deaf students, but to me, the 'good' teacher listens. She's flexible. She's supportive without hovering or being condescending. You know, I had several who had the `If you can't stand the heat, get out of the kitchen' attitude, as if I shouldn't be there if I couldn't make it in regular, prescribed fashion, and there's some wisdom to that philosophy, but I had a few teachers who were so rigid and lacking in compassion that their kind of 'heat' just wasn't anything a student should have had to live with. Only, I was too innocent and unassertive by nature to know it or deal with it at that point. So, let me describe a bad teacher or two before I clarify what makes a good one.

"I had a history teacher who called himself an S.O.B. I had to ask my friend Julie, who had an older brother, what the letters stood for, but when I found out, I knew the teacher was right on target about himself. For one thing, he had us do a debate in teams of four. Since my hearing had diminished by that time to the point where I heard very little, I nicely asked him if I might go first. I knew I would be lost in rebuttal. Well, the guy just wouldn't do it, Paige. No one reads lips well enough to see other debaters standing in front of her and facing the wrong way. I winged it, rattling off facts that didn't specifically address what had just been said, hoping I would stumble onto the right info. Of course I didn't, and the grade I got was dismal."

I just shook my head.

"Worse, he wouldn't even allow me to have another student take notes, which had been my mainstay in classes, filling in as they did the lost parts of discussion. It's not surprising that I missed some critical nuggets of history that popped up on tests. There were little fillips beyond the textual material that I couldn't possibly have anticipated or chanced upon through extra reading, yet which he expected me to know. He had also stated that he would stick to a midterm, a final, the debate, and a paper in determining our grades.

"I had to be out of school for a few days one time for medical tests in another city, and when I returned after the excused absence, to my great surprise, it was test day in history class."

"A pop quiz?"

"Worse. The other students had gotten a two-day warning about the test and were prepared. I asked the teacher if I might delay in taking it and have equal opportunity to prepare, but no, I'd happened to return right on test day, which in his eyes meant I had to take it then and there. I was so upset by his attitude and being unprepared, especially on the heels of discouraging news about my hearing, that of course I didn't do well."

I shook my head again, totally appalled. "Did you tell anyone he was being so unfair?"

"No, that's the strange thing, looking back. Or maybe it's not so odd. I was struggling to survive, and maybe I didn't make waves because so many people thought I shouldn't even be in public school. Someone had told my mom that I belonged with 'my own kind' and it sort of stuck in my mind as a threat. Remember, an interpreter wasn't an option then. But the point is some teachers' lack of sensitivity and unwillingness to make the minor modifications needed to give me as equal an educational opportunity as possible.

"I didn't make waves in college, either. When the French professor wouldn't have me because I was deaf, I just took Spanish instead, and did well in it. A good teacher is someone like my Spanish professor. She and I had talked before the first class about my by-then total hearing loss in relation to a foreign language, and from the start she had a natural sensitivity and kept her mind open about me. She dealt in what she called the nitty-gritty, which she determined from our conversations and with my approval meant my reading Spanish proficiently. To heck with my speaking it well. I did speak it, but she gently joked just to me that I sounded like someone poorly cast in a western movie. Not only was my Spanish heavily accented, it was with a French inflection left over from high school French when I still had a little hearing. I'm sure I sounded weird at best. I could read the language very well, though, and I was good enough at the grammar and exercises that I actually tutored other Spanish students. So, that's a good teacher. I learned the subject matter, but I also felt good about myself."

Tutoring students in Spanish after having been denied French was really something. I wondered if Abby had had any such opportunities. Of course, Melissa was talking about college. I thought of Abby's Mr. Jeffers and memorizing the vocabulary words list. "Did you have some like that in high school, too?"

"Maybe not quite that special, but yes, I did. I've blotted so much out from those days, but I remember bits and pieces. I'll give you an example . . . . "

The oddest thing happened then. It was as if Melissa's mind wandered and encountered something very unsettling. She stayed frozen for so long that I finally touched her arm.

"Melissa?"

When she looked at me, her eyes were wet. "I'm sorry."

"No, don't be," I said. "What's wrong?"

"I . . . I was trying to remember examples of good things from high school and good teachers, but my mind drew such a blank that it was . . . oh . . . terrifying. The Latin teacher must have been good enough. I had one math teacher who was okay. I'm sure there were many kindnesses and instances of under-standing, but they just don't come to me, and it's a total shock because I'm a positive sort of person, a person who finds good in others, so that what I'm feeling must be the sum total of my high school experience.

"I realize more than ever that it was the little, unmeant cruelties that demoralized me so much and that linger as ghosts armed with barbed little hands, ready to prod a still-tender part of me without a moment's notice. I had pushed these out of my mind, Paige, but a ghost is a ghost, ready to materialize out of nowhere."

"Maybe we should change the topic away from school."

"No, you want to understand, so let me tell you 'an after-noon in the life of' story. Abby may or may not have had such an experience, but you know, the more I think about it, the more I suspect that she did, because even the `good' teacher can be unintentionally cruel, as this one was."

Little, unmeant cruelties: I knew this was something I needed to know. "I'd like to hear about it."

"Okay. My high school was in an old brick building. I had a class on the second floor in the afternoon, followed by English in the annex, which was close to a city block away. Since students didn't carry backpacks in those days—most of us girls had a purse, and we just carried our books in the crook of one arm—I had to stop at my locker between classes to exchange books. I had to stoop down a little to rotate the lock, and the position of my body, along with sometimes getting my elbow grazed by a passing student, just made it hard. Balancing precariously, sometimes I had to try the combination three or four times. I actually had nightmares about that lock! Anyway, when I finally did get the right book, I had to navigate through scores of other students jostling all around me, down the stairs, and through a long hallway that led to the annex.

"That hallway was sheer torture. I can recall with an almost metallic taste in my mouth the fear of falling. I'd hurt myself. I'd become a laughingstock. Each possibility seemed worse than the last. As it was, I walked stiffly, sort of zombie-like, for a time after my illness, concentrating upon such things as the solid feel of the floor beneath my feet or a nice wall as an anchor. I tried to stay near a wall, in fact, so that there would be motion on one less side of me, but this wasn't always possible since there were classrooms with doors and students flowing in and out. I thought the very motion around me would topple me. Of course, I didn't walk very quickly, couldn't walk quickly, and sometimes I was late for English, which was a big deal to me. I was so shy by nature, Paige, that I had had a phobia about being late for as long as I could remember, because lateness meant calling negative attention to myself.

"Back then, English classes at my school were divided into three sections: comp for part of the year, literature for another part, and speech for the third. The class in the annex happened to be the speech requirement.

"When I eventually got there that day, everyone was

already seated, and Miss Timmerman, a woman with a very patrician face and fresh-from-the-bandbox appearance, was speaking to the class. I knew I was late, and I felt like bolting, so I had to steel myself to take center stage by walking in my stiff, post-meningitis gait. I can remember being proud of myself for conquering my shyness enough not to give in to the temptation to leave before anyone saw me, even if it meant being . . . even the word still cuts into me . . . ."

"*Tardy*," I supplied, and Melissa nodded.

"Sounds silly."

"No, and I think Abby was that way about being on time. She was shy, as well. What happened?"

"Miss Timmerman really lambasted me for being late. I still heard a little then. What she said came out only in bits and pieces, but I knew because I could see the censure like a scar on her perfect face and feel her scolding in the expression of the other students, all staring at me. I wanted to evaporate.

"But even that was small potatoes compared to her impression of my performance as a speaker and the way she announced it to everyone else."

Melissa leaned over and almost violently plucked a wilted petunia from its stem. These were old hurts, and I really felt for her. This sounded like out-and-out abuse to me and left me feeling cold. I also wondered how Abby, with pain still so fresh, had managed.

"Of course, my mother had had a conference with my teachers, the principal, and my advisor about my hearing," Melissa continued. "Remember, though, that these people had no special education background, and I don't know which ones were worse: those who thought I didn't belong, or the ones who seemed to accept that I did, only to expect me to do everything everyone else did, and just the way they did it. To some extent, then, Miss Timmerman knew.

"I had practiced my assigned speech over and over at home. My voice was clear and precise, according to my parents, who had listened to my rehearsal, but it was a living room voice,

Paige. Without hearing normally, I forgot to compensate for background noises or for the large, high-ceilinged classroom in the annex, so when I spoke, my voice was too soft. It just didn't carry.

"'Class, isn't that the worst speaking voice you've ever heard?'" she asked. I pieced together the piercing words and just died. Tears brimmed behind my eyes as I raised my voice, but I couldn't keep it up, and each time it trailed back into softness, I got a 'Melissa, you MUST learn to keep your voice up. We can't hear you, can we, class?' Lots of heads shook, so I knew it was true, and I tried even harder. My phrasings, my timing, and, of course, my enthusiasm for my topic: the intense focus upon volume blanked them out. I was so afraid of being told to speak up still again, and the ordeal seemed to stretch on like some surreal nightmare as I stood there almost visibly trembling.

"Why couldn't she have talked to me privately? Why didn't she understand that I had recently been through a medical ordeal and was lucky to even be there? So, it was a horrible, demeaning feeling, as though there were something unforgivably wrong with me, when it wasn't my fault, for heaven's sake, that I couldn't hear my own voice."

I thought of Abby's similar treatment during the biology spelling bee, and I ached for both my sister and this woman who had, at least to some extent, been belittled for a physical limitation. For an instant, Mauthausen came to mind. Had the persecution all those years ago begun that minutely and subtly? To what extent had the simple, terrible lack of compassion and nonacceptance of an individual's handicap, religion, or belief snowballed to feed a madman's frenzy? Had it even been fed by the Miss Timmermans of the time?

"She sounds like a witch," was all I said. "How did you ever get by?"

"I gritted my teeth. It's amazing that they're not stubs just from Miss Timmerman. And I cried. Oh, I cried."

I admired Melissa Black so much right then. "You deserve a gold medal."

"Thanks. I just did what I had to do. Even with laws and more awareness of deafness today, your sister may have encountered some Miss Timmermans, too. People like us are also ripe for exploitation, sometimes subtle and other times not so subtle."

"Are you thinking of anything in particular?"

"Yes, but listen to me. I've been doing all the talking."

"No, that's what I came for. Please go on."

"All right. The instance I'm thinking of happened in college, but it also occurs in high school."

"Which means it could have happened to Abby."

"I'm afraid so, yes. Mine was a definite case of sexual harassment that today would not be tolerated. At that time, with my subservient personality and no antidiscrimination laws to protect me, it was sink or swim. This guy, a biology professor, waived my laboratory science requirement without ever having talked to me about it. The funny thing is, I had done well in biology in high school and was looking forward to it in college. Still, the waiver was done, and lab courses were out at his instigation. He may have been trying to be helpful, but I felt diminished, because my motto, which had evolved in high school, had been that it's better to try and fail than never to try at all; and here was this man taking away the option that had helped me define myself since my illness.

"Well, Paige, if it had ended there, it might have been discriminatory enough, but it went much further. He also taught a course in human sexuality, and he said he would let that fulfill my science requirement. The upshot was that he insisted we approach the material on a one-to-one basis in his office. He couched it in ever-so-kind terms, as if he were sparing me a class filled with fast-paced discussion I would miss. No one took notes, he told me, since the class was designed to be fun as well as educational. So, I never went to class."

"What a jerk!"

"Oh, he was. We sat there in his office and talked about all these terribly embarrassing things. The textbook was quite graphic. I think I wrote a paper on human sexuality in ancient

Greece, but mainly he just talked about his own sexual problems, as if I needed to know. He never actually made a pass at me, but it was always there, sort of lurking in the background, and today the mere thought that anyone would subject a deaf student— any student—to this treatment infuriates me. Of course, I'm also mad at myself. But again, I feared calling attention to myself or being told I didn't belong in college."

What could I say? To have been hit upon that way because she had seemed vulnerable was unconscionable. "You were just trying to fit in."

"Too hard, maybe. Even though there are laws today to protect deaf students from out-and-out discrimination, the same attitudes that were there when I was in school still exist in some people. I'm sure your sister experienced at least a few embarrassing, belittling, upsetting instances."

I told Melissa about the biology spelling bee, and she just shook her head. Again, I wondered how many other situations Abby had faced and how she had handled them, both in actuality and emotionally. Then again, maybe the climate had been enough better for Abby that she hadn't faced as much as Melissa had.

Something puzzled me. "Did you ever think about getting out of it and going to a special school?"

"No. I knew I belonged in the public high school and, later, in college. I firmly believe that the best school for a deaf student reflects some of those variables Justin no doubt told you about, such as the age of onset of deafness. My sister-in-law was born deaf and never heard speech, for instance. She neither spoke nor depended upon lipreading, and she throve in the school for the deaf, where she fit in socially as well as educationally. She went on to become a productive citizen, successful businesswoman, wife, and mother. I have only the highest regard for her.

"But that wouldn't have been right for me. My background in my most formative years was aural/oral. I heard and spoke at the time I was learning language. Even as a young child,

I thought in words, whereas my sister-in-law, according to Justin, thought in sign symbols. I certainly don't mean this as one-upmanship, but I was reading *Moby Dick* and Chaucer at the time of my illness, and from the standpoint of a solid English base, I had educational advantages over students like my sister-in-law, although I think she may have had some emotionally. She wasn't caught in that bewildering 'before and after' situation I was in as a newly deafened person. It doesn't mean that some-one like Margaret can't master English, but there are some built-in hurdles for one who has never heard it.

"Listen to me," she interrupted herself with a smile. "I'm getting long-winded."

"No. I find this very interesting. Go on. What kinds of hurdles?"

"Well, for one thing, hearing people copy the way words sound without even thinking about it. It just happens. Language acquisition is a complicated, fascinating phenome-non. Whether one signs or speaks, though, isn't a measure of intelligence. Although visual, sign language is just another lan-guage, neither inferior nor superior to English, and what's right for the individual is a very personal matter.

"I do sign a little now to communicate with Margaret, but I enjoy words even though I don't receive them sponta-neously in the old way, and I'm very comfortable speaking . . . in my living room voice," she laughed. "Justin has sometimes called me a hearing person who just can't hear."

I smiled. "I think Abby would have stayed with speech, too. She was becoming a good lipreader. Is it *lip*reading or *speech*reading?"

"Well, to Justin it's *speech*reading. Literally, one reads speech, rather than just lips; it involves reading body language and eye contact as well as just looking at the lips. But to me it's always been *lip*reading. I do zero in on the mouth so that I can discern tongue-fronting and the other linguistic elements that distinguish one phoneme from another. In my way of thinking, either term is correct."

"Thanks. Anyway, I have a hunch that Abby would have wanted to sign a little, too. My parents seemed to fear signing as something that would take away speech."

Melissa shook her head emphatically. "Well, it doesn't. It just gives a person like Abby one more option in communicating. It's odd. I'm oral myself, but I'm not an oralist in philosophy. I think the mode of communication has to fit the child. I'm glad that I wasn't forced to sign at the expense of speaking and reading lips, but at the same time, I think the oral approach would have been dead wrong for someone like my sister-in-law or someone who has heard but doesn't master lipreading or feel comfortable with it. People get hung up on one mode as 'right' or 'wrong.' Who says? I wonder. Deaf people aren't gingerbread people cut from the same mold."

"Then even with a Miss Timmerman you felt you belonged there?"

"Oh, definitely. It's what kept me going."

"Maybe Abby didn't feel it."

"She may still have been in a daze from all that was happening. I'm not sure I developed that sense of belonging until a little later—probably partly because of the Miss Timmermans of my world—but at some point, it was just there."

I thought of the missed words, the social isolation, the discrimination, and the unintentional cruelty that Melissa had described. Had they mounted for Abby to the extent that she had felt like an outcast, and had that contributed to what happened on that last fateful day?

"Didn't you ever get depressed?" I asked.

"Did I!"

"To the extent of thinking about suicide? Oh, Melissa, I'm sorry. That's too personal. Please just forget I asked that."

"No, that's fine," she cut in. "This whole thing is personal. In high school, no, I don't remember thinking about it as a genuine possibility. I wished I were dead sometimes, but I didn't ever plan to do anything about it." She paused, and her eyes swept the deck before meeting mine again.

"When I was in college, however, I did try to kill myself. To this day, I don't know why, and I don't think it had as much to do with my deafness as my personality. I had never had the best self-esteem in the world, so it's possible that the attitudes of others exaggerated it, but I don't really know. After I had taken the sleeping pills I bought over the counter, I just knew I wanted to live, so I went for help while there was still time. I also talked to somebody later who helped me understand the emotional repercussions of losing hearing at that particular time in my life. I've had some rocky times since then, but I know I'm alive for some reason."

If only Abby had known that! Had Melissa been stronger than Abby? Luckier? What had it been? Abby had sought professional help, too, and obviously it had not worked. Although I realized that ethics called for a certain degree of silence on a doctor's part, I vowed anew to at least try to learn something about Abby's last months once Dr. Damon returned from his trip. At the very least, perhaps he could help me cope with the fact that someone so special was gone.

A small, star-shaped flower in one of Melissa's pots stared back at me, the lone blue blossom in a sea of pinks, and I thought I saw my sister for just a second. I blinked hard.

"Are you thinking about Abby?" Melissa asked softly.

"Yeah. I was just wondering what went through her mind . . . you know . . . before. Is it really that awful to be deaf?"

Melissa became so animated that the cat woke up, stretched, and gazed at us with those distinctive Siamese-blue eyes from its chair.

"No! No! A thousand times no! I didn't mean to give you that impression. The adjustment was difficult, but life is good, no less so, I have the conviction, than if I could hear, because I've made it so, let it be. I have done pretty much what I set out to do in life. It's true that I didn't become a nurse. No one would have had me in a program then. Fortunately, there are more opportunities today. I've tried, anyhow, to diversify my interests and build up my strengths. I always enjoyed fiddling around with a camera, for example, so I threw myself into learning photography as an art."

"The pictures in your husband's office?" I asked, thinking of the wonderful shots of cathedrals and chateaux.

She blushed lightly. "Mmm hmm. Mine, from our trips. More importantly, through all the struggles in high school and college, I got a lot out of my education. I have a master's in English and have done a little writing. It's true that there are no more bird chirps for me and that a movie in a theater has a lot of dialogue holes, but deafness has also opened my eyes, and I am moved beyond words at the way we can adapt to almost anything. It's just the little things."

"I never thought of the plus side of not hearing. Little things? What do you mean?"

"Well, let me think. Using the eyes in a different, fuller way, for instance. To use the movie example again, at first after I couldn't hear, when I went to see a film in the theater, I felt so abysmally cut off. Then I began seeing what I might not ordinarily have noticed: a minor stage prop, some cinematic mistake that tickled my funny bone, or the details of a certain decor. Instead of focusing upon the verbal gaps, I learned to put it all together and come up with something meaningful. Why, Justin even says that my power of observation usually leads me to hone in on a screen murderer long before he does.

"I'm a mother and a grandmother, and I worried about communicating with my own child. How would I meet her needs without hearing her words? Again, however, there are ways around not hearing that touch the soul, such as when my little girl, who just sensed my deafness almost from the start, bent down as a toddler, tugged my skirt, and looked up when she spoke her still-babyish speech so that I could *see* it. I still get choked up whenever I think of that little face and her instinctively careful enunciation. Even today, she and I have a very special relationship.

"And deafness can have pluses beyond one's wildest imagination, for it was my not hearing that led me to Justin after many years as a divorced single mother. I'm sure I never would have met him or fallen in love with him had I not been deaf, but that element actually brought us together as student and teacher. It's a special bond even now. His approach to deafness is from having had a deaf sister and from years of academic study and practical exposure in the field of the education of the deaf, while mine is from having lived one kind of deafness, so we even complement each other that way. I've opened my mind so much through having known him, Paige, and he says he has gained a certain way of seeing things from me.

"So, *becoming* deaf is horrible, but it can, and often does, lead to new perspectives, self-enrichment, and other very positive things, so that being deaf is just . . . well . . . being.

"I don't think I felt this way at Abby's age. When losses are new, you become overwhelmed by what isn't, to the extent of sometimes losing sight of what is and is yet to be. Living with so many fresh hurts, you begin to fill in the blanks with bleak scenarios.

"Paige, do you blame Abby for having taken her life?"

The question caught me off guard. "Blame her? I don't know. I guess I'm angry that she didn't value her life enough to hang in there. She was so beautiful, Melissa, outwardly and inwardly, with lots of talent and potential, and the question 'Why?' rings through my brain like a gong."

"Honey, I can't know what you are feeling. It must be excruciating to lose someone that way, especially a younger sister. I think I understand, though, on some level. You said something about Abby not valuing her life enough. Maybe she did. Maybe it was others who let her down by not valuing it enough to listen, to be receptive to her needs, and to keep an open mind. You know, if you believe in sin, I've often thought that a narrow mind is the most unacknowledged offense in the world."

"I feel so awful, feeling angry at her sometimes, Melissa."

"I think it goes along with the territory of being a survivor. You're one of the ones left behind, and you're one of the ones left to bear the brunt of the pain. But you have to let the pain work itself out and move on, and I admire you for wanting to understand what your sister's life was really like."

"A survivor. I'll remember that." Our conversation was winding down. I glanced at my watch and was shocked to see that we had been talking and sipping iced tea for close to two hours. Just as her husband hadn't, Melissa didn't seem in any hurry for me to leave, but in many ways our time together had been draining, and I knew she must feel it, too, especially, I realized almost guiltily, since she had been reading lips the whole while.

I remembered something Abby had said and para-phrased it. "Are your eyes ready to fall out?"

She laughed. "You understand!"

"To tell you the truth, you do such a remarkable job that I all but forgot that you've been using your eyes so intently. Abby used to use that expression."

"Good. You are remembering her and laughing just a little. I wish I had known her."

"And she, you."

─CHAPTER TEN─

Abby I was terrified. The broken bits and pieces of me were hurtling into a black hole of a reality that wasn't mine.

When I was little, I had a recurrent nightmare about being in a rowboat on a lake at the height of a storm. As the wind howled and the waves grew menacing, I somehow lost the scrap of old, soft nightgown that had made me feel safe. There I was, suspended on the black, bottomless waters, familiar flannel gone overboard, while the rickety, abandoned dance hall that I just knew was haunted loomed on the shore.

"It's only a dream," Mom, Dad, or Paige had always assured me.

No dream was as scary as my recent life. It was more than just waking up each morning to find that my changed state of being was reality. It wasn't just my vanishing hearing. People dragged me down. "Do this, Abby. No, do that, Abby." Their power as adults, as wise ones who ought to know some answers, had at first comforted me, but that had changed as their voices nullified mine. As my suggestions, and then pleas, wafted into nothingness, I felt trapped by a growing sense of depreciation.

Although I couldn't hear it, sometimes I felt my moan as I grasped the fact that it was another day, which meant new struggles to battle the optimists who thought I still could do anything, including hear better than I did; the pessimists who had decided that I was doomed to fail; and the microcosmic duel within myself between hope and despair. Worn down, I was beginning to doubt myself. *Hear me: Can't I be something besides a set of ears needing to be fixed?* When no one heard my cry, I tamped down my feelings and started going with the flow, which only made me feel increasingly lost, like a river whose course was being forced to change.

Gradually, I spiraled down into a state of not caring, not knowing who I was anymore. In the fight to stand up for myself, after having expended every feeling in my emotional lexicon, I finally wanted to feel nothing. Wasn't it easier to let others decide for me? Weren't they, after all, the adults, the protectors, the ones in a position to know? Maybe it was simply my fate to be recreated into the person they wanted me to be.

About the only fight left in me revolved around the hearing aid, and it was ironic that it was my fierce resistance to wearing it that led me to the two people who forever changed my life. A doctor and a teacher, one was waiting to claim my life like a cancer—slow, insidious, and devastating—while the other emerged on my horizon as a healing balm.

As usual, Mom and Dad made the fateful appointment with the new doctor without talking to me about it first. By that time, when I was sixteen, I was too beaten down by my lack of voice in anything medical to be surprised or even especially upset. My hearing was almost nonexistent, so every conversation was a nightmare, and I had essentially stopped trying.

With my parents, doctors, and most teachers still pushing the hearing aid, and with my parents coming down on me if they caught me with it off, I was lost most of the time in a world of distortion, headaches, and supreme frustration. It was still part of the trial period, they said. It was something I had to do even if it meant being so uncomfortable that my social life perished, my grades slipped, and my self-esteem plummeted. It didn't matter to anyone how good I had been getting at reading lips, and how proud of it I was. Now, assaulted by electronic hell, I was losing whatever progress I had made there. With only their communication option open—and one that wasn't working—my world had shrunk to the dimensions of a tiny, sealed box.

Let me out!

Dad said something that came through as a rumble and some hissing when first mentioning the new doctor. I had the hearing aid on, and as his voice scorched my senses like some monstrous flame, I winced and clamped my hands over my ears.

My usual "What?" died unspoken. Suddenly, I had had enough.

With a surge of old fight, I ripped off the aid and threw it hard. It didn't seem to break, since it landed on the carpet, but my parents were furious and had their "Well, if you want to be deaf" looks. I had heard of people seeing red, but in my mini-trance when I thought my frustration and anger would burst an artery, things went sort of black.

"I can't stand it anymore! I can't stand my life!" I screamed.

Dad scribbled something and pushed the paper toward me. THAT'S WHY WE WANT YOU TO SEE DR. DAMON. HE'S A PSYCHIATRIST.

Another otologist was bad enough, but a psychiatrist? Did they think I was crazy now on top of everything else?

"Of course not," Mom laughed. She had gotten good at enunciating, and without the hearing aid to distract me, I saw her words. Why wouldn't they just give me a chance to develop my skill? Dad had always been trickier because he had thin lips, but I had been making a little headway in reading his speech before the drive to make me listen wrecked things. Now, he wrote that even the most normal people benefit from a little professional help at some points in their lives, for perspective.

"Perspective?" I repeated.

He nodded and wrote: WE THINK YOU NEED SOME ABOUT YOUR HEARING LOSS.

I couldn't believe that we were back on that merry-go-round. Why was it automatically me who needed perspective, as though I were always deficient? I might have laughed if it hadn't been so sad. Now that I was putting my foot down about what was wrong for me, I suddenly needed a psychiatrist. What about all the times I had tried to talk about my feelings, all the times I had been talked over, disregarded, pooh-poohed?

"I—"

Mom's staccato tap on my arm cut me off. I had to ask her to repeat, and I finally got, "You've closed yourself off to us."

"Closed myself off . . . . " What was the use of finishing

my thought? Closed off? Yeah, sure, but it hadn't been an entirely voluntary thing. I had talked until I was blue in the face. Wouldn't talk? They hadn't listened was more like it.

And what about them? What about their perspective?

I shook my head.

"Just try it," Mom insisted.

Another note from Dad: DR. DAMON IS HIGHLY RECOMMENDED BY JIM GRACIE.

Well, that did it. Since Dr. Gracie had been Dad's mentor, his recommendation was almost an anointment. I knew at that moment that there was no getting out of going at least once.

Dr. Damon looked pretty much like any other doctor. Physically, he was about Dad's age, with tobacco brown hair dusted at the temples by just enough silver to make him look distinguished. Almost from the start, though, he was different from other doctors. For one thing, whereas their eyes had rarely met mine, Dr. Damon's gray ones locked onto mine like beams that saw into me without my having said a word.

I didn't like it.

He disarmed me almost immediately. When he spoke, it was surprisingly casual. He even came out from behind a desk that had to be at least six feet long and suggested, more from his universal gesture than from his voice, that we sit on the green leather couch.

"*Iiiii,*" he boomed. I was trying it as my parents wished, with the hearing aid on.

"I might not understand much of what you say," I explained.

"*Iiiii* . . . rumble . . . drone."

"Dr. Damon, I'm sorry, but I just didn't get that."

With no fanfare, he whipped out a pad of paper and a pen and began asking questions in writing. It was just the usual, about my age, when I got sick, and so forth, but I was sort of impressed by the way he didn't seem irritated to have to write. I answered everything politely but didn't volunteer much. He brought up topics such as school, and I told him I was taking geometry and having a hard time with it, and that I used to like writing essays.

He sometimes tried talking, and at one point, even though the sounds got in the way, I focused upon his mouth and realized that he had as perfect an enunciation as I had ever encountered. I turned off my hearing aid when he wasn't looking, and he began writing fewer notes. When I missed something, he repeated or occasionally resorted again to writing, but I think he thought I was listening instead of lipreading.

Of course, finally he said something when I wasn't looking, and he was on to me. He touched my arm to get my attention.

"You don't have your hearing aid turned on, do you?"

"What? Uh, no, no, I don't."

"Why is that?"

"Why? What difference does it make? I'm just more comfortable without it."

"You ____."

"What?" I hadn't been able to fill the gap.

"Are you sure?" he repeated.

I resented being treated like some kind of reluctant brat. "Of course I'm sure!"

"Why are you so against it?"

Hadn't I just told him that I was more comfortable without it? Was this whole thing with the psychiatrist to manipulate me into using the stupid thing? If our session hadn't been almost over, I think I would have walked out on him. As it was, anger locked in, I just ignored the question.

The strange thing was, after a few days, I started wanting to tell him in no uncertain terms just why I was through with the hearing aid, so I didn't beg not to return, as I had planned to.

We began our next session by talking about school again. Then I switched. "I'm sorry for not answering you last time about the hearing aid."

"That's all right. You certainly may do that at any point." In understanding him, there were the inevitable holes and the occasional "What?" on my part, but generally speaking, it went pretty well without the hearing aid on.

"You asked why I'm so against wearing the hearing aid. If it were just that it didn't bring in much sound, that would be one thing, but, Dr. Damon, it takes these meaningless squeaks, rustles, booms and other sounds and magnifies them into something you wouldn't believe—sounds that are just noise. Instead of helping me to hear conversations or anything useful, it just gets in my way. I've given the hearing aid a good run. It just isn't working for me. Why won't my parents believe that?"

"I don't know, Abby. Why do you think?"

If I knew, I wouldn't be asking, for crying out loud. "I don't know."

"Couldn't it be because in time you will learn to use it to your best advantage?"

"But I don't want squeaks, booms, and rustles."

"What do you want?"

A medley of precious sounds played in my mind, and I got choked up.

"You were thinking about something," he said.

"Oh, Dr. Damon, robins chirping in April, my friend Alison on the phone, and music . . . oh, music."

"Your parents tell me you were an accomplished pianist. I understand that you no longer have your piano."

"No, I don't."

He must have seen me tense up. "Let's talk about why you are so angry about that."

It was so private a feeling that I didn't want to get into it, but he locked those eyes onto mine in a way that wouldn't let the question go. From deep inside where I hurt so much, the words gushed out: "They killed my music!"

"Killed?"

"Yes, *killed.*"

"But wasn't music already dead for you, Abby, in the normal sense?"

"No, and it's alive somewhere inside me even now," I

replied in a quiet voice that belied the intensity of my feeling.

"Then what do you mean by saying that they killed it?"

"I don't think I can explain it."

"Why don't you try?"

Something made me want to. Maybe if I could just make him understand this one thing, he would also understand about the hearing aid and other things. Maybe he would be my ally.

"Well, it's just that without the piano, I can't experience music the way I did. It's only a beautiful memory, and I want more. I need more."

"You can't live in the past, however. We need to make closures at various points in our lives so that we can move ahead." I didn't get all of this on his lips, so he wrote it out for me.

I clenched my fist when I read it. Closures . . . closures? Was I really supposed to write off music because my parents had axed it for me without even talking to me about it first?

"So, you think my parents were trying to bring closure by selling the piano?"

"I don't know. What do you think?"

I think I hate it when you keep asking questions. I didn't answer, but his question must have gotten to me. A little light-bulb blinked on. They'd sold it because Mom had caught on that I played with my hearing aid turned off. The piano would still be in the living room if I had just left it on and withstood the new, awful sounds.

Closures? I glanced at Dr. Damon. How could he sit there like some self-appointed deity and even suggest closure on my music? Of all the nerve, when he, like everybody else, was trying to keep me in a limbo of saving my hearing, clinging to the dream even if it meant wearing a hearing aid that made my head hurt, didn't help in the way it should, and drove me crazy. Wasn't all the focus on my hearing living in the past?

"Is creating an illusion so wrong?" I challenged.

"The illusion of normal sound, you mean?"

"Yes."

"Aren't you fighting the way things are?"

There was that maddening question again. Dig, dig, dig. Didn't he give me any credit for having half a brain?

"Look," I said. "Do you mind if we don't talk about this anymore right now?"

"What would you like to talk about?"

Another question! He had a talent for getting under my skin. I just clammed up, as I had that first time. Maybe he would realize that we weren't getting anywhere and tell my parents that I had flunked out of therapy.

But I did return, and something changed. I never knew if it was by design or by accident, but when Dr. Damon caught me looking at a book on the corner of his desk, he started talking about it. When he saw my interest, he told me I could take it home and we'd discuss it further the next time.

That began a regular discussion of poetry, novels, and short stories. Even though he still made me mad sometimes, I grew to have a high regard for his intellect. Not only was he knowledgeable about literature, but it was refreshing beyond measure to have someone in my life whose lips were relatively easy to read, who didn't force the hearing aid on me in his office, and who was willing to repeat for me without irritation, and who was actually interested in what *I* had to say. Why, we even laughed and cried at some of the same things, and I felt myself reaching and growing through my readings and our talks about literature.

"You could major in English in college," he commented, and it opened a door, an option I had never really considered even though I had always liked English in school and reading in my spare time. Sobered, I realized that no one had ever brought up college or the future since my illness, focused as they were upon my hearing or not hearing.

Naturally, he continued to chip away at topics that got to me, like how I should wear the hearing aid when I wasn't with him. He didn't support my desire to get my piano back, either. I still grew silent about some things, but I at least made an effort to open up more just so that I could get to the "dessert" of the session: the literary element.

He also suggested I begin keeping a "feelings" journal, which I did.

A strange thing happened. I could hardly wait to get to his office. I started feeling alive again, and the week's "Dr. Damon novel" or "Dr. Damon poem" carried me through six days of hurts in between. The diary, which was just for me, he said, also helped me to get back in touch.

But he didn't think I was opening up enough.

"There is something I want to discuss with you, Abby," he said after our literary moment one day several weeks into our sessions. I felt uneasy. He had gone from laughing at a humorous short story to such seriousness.

I hoped it wasn't the hearing aid again. Was he going to pressure me into wearing it at his office and spoil things? I had talked to him at length about that, trying to explain, too, how I wanted to go for awhile without it in all settings. Why shouldn't I, I argued, be throwing my effort into reading lips or anything else to avoid being drained by trying to cope with all the discordant sounds that impeded, rather than helped, communication? He listened, but mostly he just stuck with the idea that maybe I wasn't trying hard enough to accept the situation and that some of it might be something psychological that we could work through together. He had also talked to my parents and the otologist, so he reminded me that it was probably best to keep the remaining nerve stimulated. At that point, when all I heard was the noise of speech, rather than the words, I certainly couldn't fathom why. But at least Dr. Damon had let me keep it off during our sessions, and I had gotten better and better at understanding him.

And now he had something to discuss with me. Would he try to force me into keeping it on? I was sick of the hearing aid topic. Still, it didn't keep me from asking, "Oh . . . what is it?"

"I have given this a lot of thought. Abby, I think we should consider terminating our sessions. We are getting in a lot of talk about literature, but we are not making progress with the issues that brought you here in the first place."

Terminate: my heart skipped a beat at the word. Even though Dr. Damon had bugged me, just the thought of ending it, and especially breaking the connection I felt as we talked about books, shot an almost paralyzing dread through me. What was he talking about? I needed this!

All of a sudden, it hit me what I would be missing. The literature was more than words on paper or even ideas, since in it, I had actually found a substitute for my music. Oh, I still felt the aching absence of it in my life, and I wanted my piano back, but I saw in that instant that fiction was touching me in ways that paralleled the way music had. Like music, literature had brushed the divine in me in a certain way, by making me consider the great issues of human existence and relate to them in my own unique way.

In the literary voices of others, I was finding an answering call embedded within the depths of me. It was an "I've been there; I've done that" sensation because what I read reflected not just a story or events but the human condition. Why, just two weeks ago, Dr. Damon and I had talked about a Stephen Crane short story featuring a little open boat on perilous seas, ready to be capsized at a moment's notice even after a long, valiant struggle. Do we as humans keep on rowing, tired and almost sure to be swamped? Is it noble or foolish to continue fighting in the face of odds beyond our control? Questions like that set me on fire because usually, I came to see, there is no single right answer.

"Issues?" I finally asked. "Like my hearing, you mean?"

"Not your hearing. The way you deal with your hearing loss."

"I'm doing my best."

"Are you?"

"Yes. Can't we talk about Finley Peter Dunne?"

He smiled. "For now, all right."

Even though we got into a discussion of the Irish-dialect humorist and one of his "Mr. Dooley" stories, my heart wasn't in it this time. The word *terminate* reverberated through my mind and shook me to my toes.

I knew at that moment that, especially after having felt so cut off, I would do anything to keep the connection.

And he must have known that, too.

my little rehearsed speech had frittered away. Since then, I had spoken to him on the phone, but just to fill him in about what had happened to my sister. I glanced at him now. He was waiting. I had to come up with something, had to get beyond this for his sake so that he could move on.

I led him into the living room, but tense now, he didn't sit down. Still not sure what to say, I began tentatively. "I'm sorry I let so much time pass. I've been wiped out . . . consumed, really, by needing to find some answers to what happened."

"Frankly, I don't get it."

"Get what?"

"I can understand how horrible this must be for you and your family, but what about me? What about us? I thought we had something going. I thought you needed me, but you didn't even bother to return my calls. What's going on?"

Surprised by his tone and struck by the knowledge that I had completely forgotten to call him back, I couldn't meet his eyes. "I'm sorry, Kent. I—"

"It's another man, isn't it?"

Inaudibly I hoped, I sucked in my breath. Something undeniable was happening between Mark Friedell and me, but I didn't want "another man" to become the issue in Kent's mind. Mark or no Mark, regardless of what developed between us, the bottom line was that Kent Gwinner wasn't the man for me. I had, after all, been on the verge of breaking it off with him when the precipitate message about Abby had suspended me almost in midsentence.

But while Mark wasn't the main reason, I had to admit that my feelings for him had shown me what was missing with Kent and sealed my resolution to end his aspiration for a future as more than friends. This talk would have been so much simpler in pre-Mark days! Would it make it easier or harder for Kent if I told him that, yes, I had met someone else? Maybe he could accept another man more than the other, for how does a woman tell a man in love with her that what she feels is special, but sisterly, without shredding his emotions? What a novice I was at something like this.

When I spoke, it was on the heels of an involuntary sigh. "Oh, Kent . . . . "

"Do I make you that exasperated?"

"No, of course not. You know I value your friendship."

"Well, I thought you did."

I didn't like this sparring and just wanted to get on with it. I had already waited too long. "That evening in my apartment before I listened to the message on my machine I was trying to tell you something."

"That there was someone else," he finished for me.

"No. No, there wasn't another man, Kent."

"But there is now."

"Would you just let me talk? This is hard enough."

"Then why don't you just tell me?"

"I'm trying to." His interruptions were irritating, but I didn't want that emotion to sidetrack me from my goal of telling Kent what I had to as honestly and as painlessly as possible. I changed my tone. "Look, it's just that I realized even before my sister died that you deserve so much more than I can give you."

"And what, pray tell, is it you think I need?" The challenge voiced, the gears in his mind seemed to shift, and he reached for my hand. "Paige, don't you know you're what I need? You are everything a man could hope for." He looked at me with his clear gray eyes as he had so many times in the week or two preceding my decision to break it off, with a soft seeking, and I could almost hear the erratic thump of his heartbeat.

"You have to know how very, very fond of you I am," I said. "What I think you deserve is someone who can commit to you fully."

His hand in mine had grown clammy. I felt it slip away. "And you can't? I thought we had a lot in common. I thought we had everything going for us."

"We do have a lot in common, and I think we have a solid friendship, but something is just . . . missing."

"'Missing? What do you mean, `missing'?"

"I just don't feel the way . . . well . . . the way I should."

"So this is it? Is that what you are saying?"

"No, not at all. I would like always for us to be friends."

He laughed mirthlessly. "Friends? What a dunce you must think I am for walking you past those ring displays."

It was the ring thing, even though he did it lightly, that had made me fully aware that his feelings had blossomed into something far more than the friendship I felt for him. I had let finishing term papers and taking finals get in the way of saying what I needed to be fair to him. Then Abby had died, and I couldn't handle it on top of the rent in my life that had brought. Watching him now, I wished I could go back and do it differently and more fairly.

"No way are you a dunce," I said.

"Friends," he said again, shaking his head. "Well, I'll have to think about that."

I hadn't realized how the "unfinishedness" of the thing with Kent had been hanging over my head until after our conversation was over and I knew that everything was out in the open and we were both free, either as friends or not, to get on with our lives.

I was with Mark, who was eating a bacon cheeseburger at McMenamins one late afternoon and having trouble keeping the sauce from dripping.

"That tuna looks more manageable," he laughed. When he wiped his lips, I thought of our kiss and hoped the glow I felt wasn't making me stand out like a firefly. It was a weird time to think of Kent, but I did, sincerely hoping that someday he would meet a woman who glowed just for him.

I took a bite of my sandwich, and a glob of filling fell out. It was my turn to chuckle. "Oops. You spoke too soon."

"Messy but delicious."

As I nodded and took another bite of my sandwich, my thoughts returned to the interviews we had just had with Abby's school counselor and English teacher. "To change the subject,

Mark, I really appreciate the way you set up those appointments. Both Mrs. Faure and Mr. Jeffers couldn't have been nicer, even when I must have seemed from the Dark Ages not to have known what an IEP is. Oh, no, I forget exactly what the acronym stands for."

"Individualized Education Plan."

"Thanks."

It had been entirely new ground for me. The counselor had explained that such plans are designed to ensure that each student, regardless of disability, has the opportunity to reach a certain level of academic performance. After testing to determine where the student is at present, according to Mrs. Faure, the IEP becomes almost a blueprint formulating long-term goals and delineating short-range objectives in a team effort among teachers, support staff, parents, and the student herself.

Mark took a swig of cold beer, which no doubt tasted as good to him on this sizzling summer day as my iced tea did to me. When he set down his glass he said, "You seemed blown away that your parents had nixed one for Abby."

"Oh, you said it, and I was just as surprised that Mrs. Faure, although happy enough to give me the basics, seemed relieved when we moved on to the next topic. Why wouldn't anyone want an IEP? From what she said, it sounds like such a positive thing."

"It is positive. Jane was being circumspect. Like most things in life, there's another side to the story. Now, remember, I'm only a humble music teacher, not in special ed, but I know enough to be able to tell you that students like Abby are recruited."

"Recruited?"

"Yeah. You see, each child with an IEP brings money in to the state and school district, so sometimes people at schools push the IEP so that they can draw a student into the system. Naturally, they may have a vested interest since their jobs depend upon having a sufficient number of students.

"This isn't to say that most students who have IEPs don't require them. For the student who needs close monitoring and a blend of regular and special classes, which probably defines most of them, the IEP is a great boon and quite effective. It's just that kids like Abby can go either way. It depends so much upon the nature of the disability, the child's background, emotional maturity, and other factors. In other words, some students do just fine without one and, perhaps, should be left alone, sinking or swimming just like their non-IEP peers.

"As for your parents, they may have wanted Abby to have options they feared the IEP process might take away."

I supposed that made sense. Dr. Black had told me "maybe and maybe not" when I had asked if Abby had belonged in special ed, so perhaps the same held true for the IEP.

"Well," I said, "Mr. Jeffers certainly thought that Abby was doing well academically."

"Except for brief lapses when she was out for medical tests, she wasn't falling behind in any of her other classes, either, according to Mrs. Faure."

I shook my head.

"What's wrong?" Mark asked.

"Oh, I was just thinking of Mr. Jeffers and the way his praise of Abby the student was colored by the other." My sister's English teacher had perceived her as someone troubled. Although her grades never faltered significantly, Mr. Jeffers had noted a "lost look" two or three months before her death. When he had approached her about it, however, she had been uncommunicative. Then, just when he was on the brink of talking about it with Abby's counselor, it looked as if the depression was gone. She seemed elated, even radiant, and he had assumed that whatever it was that had been bothering her had taken care of itself.

"The mood swing?"

I nodded, chilled by more than the air-conditioning and my iced tea. I had read the signs of impending suicide in magazines over the years, never dreaming that I would be thinking of them in such a personal, tragic way, but one of those markers, on the heels of what Abby's teacher had said, came back hauntingly:

that sometimes there was a resignation, a seeming happiness, once the depressed person had made the decision to take definitive action.

And there I'd been, away at school, when if I hadn't been so selfish as to have needed some space, I might have been in the next bedroom and onto whatever my sister was facing.

The funky, party atmosphere of the restaurant was suddenly more than I could bear. "Let's get out of here, Mark."

When his eyes met mine, they uplifted me by their understanding, and when he simply paid the bill without a word, I knew I was falling head over heels in love with Mark Friedell.

—CHAPTER ELEVEN—

I was finding little pieces of Abby's life in information that included the words and perceptions of others. Like the hundreds of tile samples in the store where I worked, with thousands of design possibilities, so were the shards of information I gathered and stored away in my mind, not knowing which piece might somehow later fit into whatever mosaic the totality of them suggested.

What I realized, increasingly, was that if comprehension is the heart of social interaction, then having any interference with it at all must have an astonishing impact upon one's life. I had only to think of Melissa Black to be aware of the exclusion, the humiliation, and the gamut of situations and emotions that short-circuited interaction could bring. Had it gathered into a dark, impossible cloud for Abby?

I sighed. It always came back to the deafness.

I brought home books on the topic, and in them I found a world of fascinating information, but they didn't describe the Abby I had known. They talked about the Deaf as a culture, the deaf community, sign language, and issues that didn't relate as directly to my sister as many "hearing" issues did. Still convinced that not hearing was at the root of her suicide, I even threw myself into a study of language in general, in the hope that I might chance upon a key as to what she had lived, or lived without, on a daily basis.

Abby had never been handicapped from the standpoint of learning the English language. Through the dynamics of hearing it, her infant babble had developed into broad sound patterns, and she had assigned arbitrary but standardized meanings to particular things: a *kitty* was a cat, not a dog, although for a time it might have been a *meow* or a *ditty*. In the logical procession of acquiring an aural/oral language, Abby had learned the accepted grammar: *Where kitty? All gone kitty? Many kitties leaved. Many cats left. Many of the cats have left.*

That she hadn't been prelingually deaf kept it spontaneous. Spontaneity: I got a glimmer as to why Melissa's sister-in-law had been more comfortable signing. Abby, however, knew the language, knew the grammar, knew all her hearing peers did (and maybe even a bit more since she had truly loved English). The realm of meaning was hers, but the words that represented ideas and things sometimes simply had not gotten to her, either for lack of hearing them or seeing them on someone's lips.

How frustrating that must have been for her! What do you do? Do you yank a child like Abby out of her milieu? Do you replace all her words with sign symbols, all her hearing friends with deaf substitutes?

The more I looked into books, and even just at dictionaries for a definition of *language*, the more I thought how like love it is, with no pat answer because it is perceived individually. Regardless of the exact definition, though, what I came away with was the idea that although all languages may have certain properties, such as being learned, the mental process of learning one is phenomenal, a rough magic we perhaps don't think twice about unless we study linguistics or have something like deafness interfere with its spontaneous acquisition. Even then, the need for language is so great that the human spirit adapts by inventing and substituting complete, efficient visual systems.

I appreciated American Sign Language as a beautiful language unto itself, but what if you were like Abby? What if English were already your frame of reference? No, it went beyond communication mode and mechanics—the hearing aid, the degree of sound coming in or not getting through—and into an area that struck the core of who Abby was. There wasn't anything wrong with being deaf, but was there something wrong with trying to keep one's identity as, perhaps, a hearing person who no longer happened to hear?

I wasn't sure. In not knowing, I opened a totally unexpected door: the idea of getting my master's degree in the education of the deaf in a program like Justin Black's.

Taking some of the books on deafness back to the library one day, I ran into Alison and felt my heart constrict as for just a second, I seemed to see the petite Chinese-American and my Swedish-blonde sister checking out *Nancy Drew* books at ten. When I shook my head slightly, Abby disappeared, and Alison was by herself.

In the grip of the way it was and should still be, I waved at my sister's best friend. Her initial, automatic smile, though, slipped away to be replaced by a mask of pain that matched my own, and I sensed that, for now at least, I was too much a reminder of her lost friend to be of any comfort. I understood when she walked on by, but the chance encounter bothered me to the extent that I called Alison's mother, who assured me that although her daughter was hurting, she was seeing someone to help her handle her loss, which I knew probably still included some of that anger and guilt I had seen at her house.

I guessed the books, the nuggets of information about my sister, and my work at the tile shop were my therapy; I kept busy.

I had just returned from work one afternoon when the doorbell rang. It had been one of those better-than-usual days because I had had a hand in helping a young couple select a Delft polychrome tile scheme for their kitchen backsplashes. Their obvious delight in each other, their new home, and the tile was infectious, and I think I had smiled more that afternoon than at any other time since Abby's death.

Now with the ring of the bell, I thought it must be Mark to round out the day. It was funny how there had grown to be a completeness to any day that included a call or visit with him.

"Coming," I called.

I swung the door open and felt my expression change from anticipation to surprise. I hadn't seen him since he had put me on the plane bringing me back home for what turned out to be Abby's funeral. He looked so solid and familiar, this friend of mine, but finding him on the doorstep two thousand miles from his own environment was just about the last thing I had expected.

"Kent!"

"I wish you could see your face."

"It's just . . . . How did you get away?"

He grinned. "Even med students get a break now and then, believe it or not. Aren't you going to ask me in?"

"Of course."

In the foyer as I closed the door, he looked into my eyes almost questioningly and pulled me to him. He smelled the same, like an October afternoon with just a hint of smoke and spice, and memories of wind-whipped walks by the lake, shopping on State Street, and a day trip to Indiana to get away from Chicago's hustle and bustle flooded back. How many mnemonic devices had I helped him learn for things like the nerves of the body, and how many Spanish phrases had he untangled for me? It had been give-and-take and then meeting on common ground as we had laughed until our sides split at a Laurel and Hardy festival or become indignant when an adopted toddler was given back to her biological mother. In his arms now, for just a moment, I felt safe and sheltered by those common threads and genuine affection.

Then, unbidden, thoughts of Mark's embrace floated into my consciousness. Maybe Kent felt me stiffen. When we pulled apart, there was sadness in his eyes. "I feel you slipping away from me, Paige."

What he didn't realize was that I hadn't slipped away. I had never been his, never felt close in the way he had imagined. He was bright, kind, and funny, and I had enjoyed his company and even hoped it might work out, but for me some crucial element just wasn't there.

What was it I had planned to tell him that evening in Chicago, anyway? It seemed like so long ago now. In the weeks since my world had turned upside-down, the careful words of my little rehearsed speech had frittered away. Since then, I had spoken to him on the phone, but just to fill him in about what had happened to my sister. I glanced at him now. He was waiting. I had to come up with something, had to get beyond this for his sake so that he could move on.

I led him into the living room, but tense now, he didn't sit down. Still not sure what to say, I began tentatively. "I'm sorry I let so much time pass. I've been wiped out . . . consumed, really, by needing to find some answers to what happened."

"Frankly, I don't get it."

"Get what?"

"I can understand how horrible this must be for you and your family, but what about me? What about us? I thought we had something going. I thought you needed me, but you didn't even bother to return my calls. What's going on?"

Surprised by his tone and struck by the knowledge that I had completely forgotten to call him back, I couldn't meet his eyes. "I'm sorry, Kent. I—"

"It's another man, isn't it?"

Inaudibly I hoped, I sucked in my breath. Something undeniable was happening between Mark Friedell and me, but I didn't want "another man" to become the issue in Kent's mind. Mark or no Mark, regardless of what developed between us, the bottom line was that Kent Gwinner wasn't the man for me. I had, after all, been on the verge of breaking it off with him when the precipitate message about Abby had suspended me almost in midsentence.

But while Mark wasn't the main reason, I had to admit that my feelings for him had shown me what was missing with Kent and sealed my resolution to end his aspiration for a future as more than friends. This talk would have been so much simpler in pre-Mark days! Would it make it easier or harder for Kent if I told him that, yes, I had met someone else? Maybe he could accept another man more than the other, for how does a woman tell a man in love with her that what she feels is special, but sisterly, without shredding his emotions? What a novice I was at something like this.

When I spoke, it was on the heels of an involuntary sigh. "Oh, Kent . . . . "

"Do I make you that exasperated?"

"No, of course not. You know I value your friendship."

"Well, I thought you did."

I didn't like this sparring and just wanted to get on with it. I had already waited too long. "That evening in my apartment before I listened to the message on my machine I was trying to tell you something."

"That there was someone else," he finished for me.

"No. No, there wasn't another man, Kent."

"But there is now."

"Would you just let me talk? This is hard enough."

"Then why don't you just tell me?"

"I'm trying to." His interruptions were irritating, but I didn't want that emotion to sidetrack me from my goal of telling Kent what I had to as honestly and as painlessly as possible. I changed my tone. "Look, it's just that I realized even before my sister died that you deserve so much more than I can give you."

"And what, pray tell, is it you think I need?" The challenge voiced, the gears in his mind seemed to shift, and he reached for my hand. "Paige, don't you know you're what I need? You are everything a man could hope for." He looked at me with his clear gray eyes as he had so many times in the week or two preceding my decision to break it off, with a soft seeking, and I could almost hear the erratic thump of his heartbeat.

"You have to know how very, very fond of you I am," I said. "What I think you deserve is someone who can commit to you fully."

His hand in mine had grown clammy. I felt it slip away. "And you can't? I thought we had a lot in common. I thought we had everything going for us."

"We do have a lot in common, and I think we have a solid friendship, but something is just . . . missing."

"'Missing? What do you mean, `missing'?"

"I just don't feel the way . . . well . . . the way I should."

"So this is it? Is that what you are saying?"

"No, not at all. I would like always for us to be friends."

He laughed mirthlessly. "Friends? What a dunce you must think I am for walking you past those ring displays."

It was the ring thing, even though he did it lightly, that had made me fully aware that his feelings had blossomed into something far more than the friendship I felt for him. I had let finishing term papers and taking finals get in the way of saying what I needed to be fair to him. Then Abby had died, and I couldn't handle it on top of the rent in my life that had brought. Watching him now, I wished I could go back and do it differently and more fairly.

"No way are you a dunce," I said.

"Friends," he said again, shaking his head. "Well, I'll have to think about that."

I hadn't realized how the "unfinishedness" of the thing with Kent had been hanging over my head until after our con-versation was over and I knew that everything was out in the open and we were both free, either as friends or not, to get on with our lives.

I was with Mark, who was eating a bacon cheeseburger at McMenamins one late afternoon and having trouble keeping the sauce from dripping.

"That tuna looks more manageable," he laughed. When he wiped his lips, I thought of our kiss and hoped the glow I felt wasn't making me stand out like a firefly. It was a weird time to think of Kent, but I did, sincerely hoping that someday he would meet a woman who glowed just for him.

I took a bite of my sandwich, and a glob of filling fell out. It was my turn to chuckle. "Oops. You spoke too soon."

"Messy but delicious."

As I nodded and took another bite of my sandwich, my thoughts returned to the interviews we had just had with Abby's school counselor and English teacher. "To change the subject,

Mark, I really appreciate the way you set up those appointments. Both Mrs. Faure and Mr. Jeffers couldn't have been nicer, even when I must have seemed from the Dark Ages not to have known what an IEP is. Oh, no, I forget exactly what the acronym stands for."

"Individualized Education Plan."

"Thanks."

It had been entirely new ground for me. The counselor had explained that such plans are designed to ensure that each student, regardless of disability, has the opportunity to reach a certain level of academic performance. After testing to determine where the student is at present, according to Mrs. Faure, the IEP becomes almost a blueprint formulating long-term goals and delineating short-range objectives in a team effort among teachers, support staff, parents, and the student herself.

Mark took a swig of cold beer, which no doubt tasted as good to him on this sizzling summer day as my iced tea did to me. When he set down his glass he said, "You seemed blown away that your parents had nixed one for Abby."

"Oh, you said it, and I was just as surprised that Mrs. Faure, although happy enough to give me the basics, seemed relieved when we moved on to the next topic. Why wouldn't anyone want an IEP? From what she said, it sounds like such a positive thing."

"It is positive. Jane was being circumspect. Like most things in life, there's another side to the story. Now, remember, I'm only a humble music teacher, not in special ed, but I know enough to be able to tell you that students like Abby are recruited."

"Recruited?"

"Yeah. You see, each child with an IEP brings money in to the state and school district, so sometimes people at schools push the IEP so that they can draw a student into the system. Naturally, they may have a vested interest since their jobs depend upon having a sufficient number of students.

"This isn't to say that most students who have IEPs don't require them. For the student who needs close monitoring and a blend of regular and special classes, which probably defines most of them, the IEP is a great boon and quite effective. It's just that kids like Abby can go either way. It depends so much upon the nature of the disability, the child's background, emotional maturity, and other factors. In other words, some students do just fine without one and, perhaps, should be left alone, sinking or swimming just like their non-IEP peers.

"As for your parents, they may have wanted Abby to have options they feared the IEP process might take away."

I supposed that made sense. Dr. Black had told me "maybe and maybe not" when I had asked if Abby had belonged in special ed, so perhaps the same held true for the IEP.

"Well," I said, "Mr. Jeffers certainly thought that Abby was doing well academically."

"Except for brief lapses when she was out for medical tests, she wasn't falling behind in any of her other classes, either, according to Mrs. Faure."

I shook my head.

"What's wrong?" Mark asked.

"Oh, I was just thinking of Mr. Jeffers and the way his praise of Abby the student was colored by the other." My sister's English teacher had perceived her as someone troubled. Although her grades never faltered significantly, Mr. Jeffers had noted a "lost look" two or three months before her death. When he had approached her about it, however, she had been uncommunicative. Then, just when he was on the brink of talking about it with Abby's counselor, it looked as if the depression was gone. She seemed elated, even radiant, and he had assumed that whatever it was that had been bothering her had taken care of itself.

"The mood swing?"

I nodded, chilled by more than the air-conditioning and my iced tea. I had read the signs of impending suicide in magazines over the years, never dreaming that I would be thinking of them in such a personal, tragic way, but one of those markers, on the heels of what Abby's teacher had said, came back hauntingly:

that sometimes there was a resignation, a seeming happiness, once the depressed person had made the decision to take definitive action.

And there I'd been, away at school, when if I hadn't been so selfish as to have needed some space, I might have been in the next bedroom and onto whatever my sister was facing.

The funky, party atmosphere of the restaurant was suddenly more than I could bear. "Let's get out of here, Mark."

When his eyes met mine, they uplifted me by their understanding, and when he simply paid the bill without a word, I knew I was falling head over heels in love with Mark Friedell.

—Chapter Twelve—

Abby The literary connection I was finding in those sessions with Dr. Damon didn't exactly make me happy, but it helped me to get through each day by giving me something to focus upon besides my hearing loss and all the flak from the people around me. I finally had something to look forward to. There was movement in my life where there had only been stagnation. There was even hope for a future that didn't look entirely bleak. So, even though my hearing situation was no better, some of my old enthusiasm for school returned. Still afraid that he might terminate our sessions and I would lose that special sanctuary where I had a voice, permission to keep the hearing aid off, and where a world of new hope and ideas abounded, I even made a deal with myself to give the hearing aid one last try, and compromised by keeping it on for as long as I could stand it in school.

That I knew I had him and the literary connection to thank for the slight upswing in my life made me vulnerable, although I didn't fully realize it at the time. I just knew I couldn't —wouldn't!—lose it. He saw it, too, and moved right in with what he called an accepted aspect of therapy.

I don't know what would have happened—or not happened—if Dr. Damon's dog hadn't gotten run over, because it showed me a side of him that I had never seen: He was as susceptible to pain as everyone else; he was human, and I felt for him. He was basically so inscrutable that I had sometimes wondered if his reactions and comments were only educated opinion or impersonal observation, rather than deep-down emotion. Maybe something like his wonder at the sorry plight of a literary character had been the real man showing through, after all.

The real person certainly surfaced now, and I felt a rush of something indefinable, almost a feeling of triumph tinged by tenderness, to see this chink in his professional armor. Why, he had tears in his eyes!

I couldn't help asking, "Is anything wrong, Dr. Damon?"

He swallowed hard. "Oh, my Yorkshire terrier, Maude, was hit by a car this morning. There wasn't anything we could do." He had to repeat, but as always, he did so without irritation.

"I'm so sorry. I hope she didn't suffer."

"Thank you. No, I don't think she did. At least we had one last good romp together at the cabin this past weekend." The vacation home on Mt. Hood, he explained, had been Maude's favorite spot. "She would make a beeline for the creek, splash in in wild abandon, and then come out looking and smelling like a drowned rat. How she loved that!"

It was strange to think of Dr. Damon outside this room. For the first time, I considered that he had a life: a dog he obviously loved, a cabin . . . what else? When I focused back upon him, he looked uncustomarily sad, staring vacantly as he was at the blotter on his desk. Marbled by such evident feelings, this man suddenly bonded to me in a new way. I wanted to reach out to him.

"Is there anything I can do? Maybe we should scrap today's session," I offered.

His eyes brushed mine, and a current of understanding passed between us. "That's not necessary, although I appreciate your offer. She was just a dog, after all."

"I'm not sure I believe that 'just a dog' business. François, my poodle, died when I was twelve, and I remember the hole his absence left. He was a very important part of our family."

"You're very kind and helpful."

"Not as helpful as you've been to me." The rest just popped out: "Dr. Damon, our literary discussions mean the world to me. You won't really terminate, will you?"

"I don't want to."

"The way you say that frightens me."

"We need some forward movement," he said as he walked from behind his desk and sat on its edge, facing me. His aftershave lotion wafted into my nostrils and made me think of some exotic tropical island. He reached for my hand and took it so lightly that I could hardly believe it was happening. Dr. Damon holding my hand? My first instinct was to pull it from him, but I left it there, feeling its not unpleasant warmth, and he continued speaking. "You need to delve into your heart of hearts, your soul, and share with me in a way that you are not. Abby, I sincerely want to help you, and I know that I can if you will let me."

"But you are. I—"

"Shh. We are only scratching the surface."

"Then how?"

"What do you feel when I touch your hand?"

"Feel? I don't know. A little uncomfortable, to be honest."

"Why is that?"

I shrugged.

"Couldn't it be because it makes you feel like confiding?"

"I don't know," I repeated.

"There is an accepted aspect of therapy that involves touching as a stepping stone to the kinds of revelations I think would benefit you."

He still had my hand within his grasp. Touching: Was holding my hand what he meant? I could do that. His warmth flowed into me, binding us together somehow.

"Revelations?"

"About life. Especially about yourself, Abby. You need to find out who you are now that your life is colored by hearing loss, people with changed or changing attitudes toward you, and your unique set of frustrations, fears, limitations, and strengths. You need to redefine yourself, and perhaps that starts with trusting me completely, so that you can later transfer that full trust to yourself."

He'd hit upon something. Hadn't my belief in myself swirled into the nebulous somewhere where so much of me had disappeared? What if this was my chance to be whole again, to be happy? He must know what he was doing. I glanced at the diplomas and all the awards on the walls and thought of the times I had seen his picture in the newspaper as he spearheaded still another philanthropic cause. His credentials were sterling. Why, according to Dad, Dr. Damon had actually walked out onto the ledge of a twenty-story building to "talk down" a suicidal patient. He went the extra mile.

He dropped my hand. "I don't want to terminate our sessions, Abby, but I'm not the therapist for you if you can't trust me, and I'll be happy to refer you to a colleague if you can't do that and decide to terminate."

There was that ugly word again: *terminate*. My heart constricted as novelists and poets, humorists and short story writers —all their ideas, their inspiration, their food for thought— sprang to mind and I realized all over again what I would be missing without him, my literary guide.

In a recess of my mind, my post-meningitis screams reverberated. As I shook my head to free it from the echo of my agony, images of being sick and its aftermath flashed before me:
   —the headache
   —the coma
   —the onset of incessant struggling
It came to just nine hundred days . . .
   —hearing going up and down, frittering away
   —drug reactions
   —the hearing aid
Only nine hundred days . . .
   —parents turned into aliens
   —teachers being overly solicitous or even cruel
   —severed friendships
   —doctors ignoring all but my hearing
Just days piled onto days . . .
   —embarrassment and humiliation
   —lost music, conversations . . . normality
   —my silenced voice and no control
   —all gone . . . me.
I wanted to explode and break through the darkness of

those nine hundred days like a circus performer rushing into the light from the depths of a cannon. But wasn't Dr. Damon already showing me the way, if slowly? Maybe we weren't talking about some of the issues he wanted to, or thought we should be addressing, but wasn't it enough that he had given me the promise of brighter days in the proof that someone would actually listen to me, in encouragement that included aiming for college, and, of course, in the vital link through literature to something . . . something I couldn't quite put my finger on, but which I sensed was a sliver of a better self?

Touching . . . . Where did that fit into the picture?

Like a seesaw, what I thought were the only options carried me back and forth, back and forth: trusting him completely even though some hazy instinct cautioned me against it, or risking getting lost once again in the miasma of the endless, murky nine hundred days and having them engulf me for what could be the rest of my life.

In the end, there was no contest. I had to save myself, and as I saw it, that hinged upon my need for him. Wasn't Dr. Damon the only one who was exposing me to new, good facets of myself, the only one who saw the whole me and not just my ears? With the word *trust* as my beacon, and the intense fear of the nine hundred days stretching into dark eternity, I moved toward the light as a moth to the flame.

Therapy or not, I had to shut off some of my feelings to be able to handle the new, very personal dimension of our time together, for the touching turned out to be far more than hand-holding. The internal seesaw ride became even wilder: *This is wrong; I'm bad/No, I'm saving myself, so it must be okay* . . . back and forth, back and forth, until the turmoil nearly made me vomit. I let the word throb inside my skull every time he touched me: I had to trust, to trust, to trust . . . .

Although the conflict inside of me continued, gradually I decided that his approach must be right. Like a morning glory at dawn, I felt myself opening to the world around me as through literature, he presented an unending array of variations on the great themes of human existence, which, in turn, brought me stirrings of self-discovery and a renewed tie to the rest of humankind. I even started talking about things like my parents, my fear of going completely deaf, and options for the future.

Acquiring these new insights had an unexpected downside. One day at school, for example, a wave of sadness washed over me as I saw Jay Cassidy and realized that my relationship with Dr. Damon had destroyed something forever. How sweet my fantasies had been about Jay: the dance, the first kiss, the big white wedding where I would wear pearls and blush and share cake with him on that most perfect of days. In my mind, carefree and innocently, we had run through meadows, he and I, and his smile had touched a corner of my spirit so very gently. That day at school, though, marked the beginning of a new recognition: with something precious lost, it hurt to even meet Jay's eyes.

Still, Dr. Damon opened a world of hope, a panoply of tomorrows, and the feeling I came away with time and again was simply that, despite the detractions of our relationship, I couldn't ever again let myself be trapped inside the box of today where I just plodded through sixty joyless minutes of every hour.

Seesaw, seesaw . . . healing, hurting; right, wrong . . . .

It was at this point that the teacher who forever changed my life reentered it unexpectedly.

One day after my last period class, Alison wasn't in the school music room with her violin as she thought she might be. "Look for me but don't wait if I'm not there," she'd said. The piano was there, though, looming and large, inviting and repelling. Literature may have become a substitute of sorts, but, ah, the spell a piano could still cast over me! If I hadn't gotten sick, I knew I would have liked this room the way I had the music room in junior high just before my illness. I had felt so at home there, so wanted, and so crucial to our modest orchestra.

That hadn't happened in this room. I was a stranger here, and struck to the core by a feeling of not belonging and a longing so intense that I could almost taste it, I turned to leave.

I almost made it out, but some irresistible force pulled

me back. Trancelike, I sat down on the piano bench. Oh, the familiar hardness of it! Simultaneously, I felt powerful and as helpless as a newborn kitten, so I just sat there, watching the eighty-eight keys stretch like a stairway to infinity, both beckoning and forbidding as my fingers lay paralyzed in my lap.

Memories kaleidoscoped: Mom playing *Harbor Lights* clumsily; Madame Marek counting *ein, zwei, drei*; and me through the years, painstakingly learning scales and études, getting passages just right, and playing, playing, playing with wonderful sensations radiating through me. I had felt so whole then, and happy.

I don't know for how long I sat there staring at the keyboard, but I came out of my reverie shocked to find that my right hand had come to life. I looked in astonishment as I saw it poised over the keys. Then my left hand moved, and as if they had a mind of their own, they began playing softly. For one shining moment, it felt so right and healing.

Then the noise rushed through my hearing aid, piercing my senses and leaving that old wound gaping. Discordant sound ringing through my brain, my hands flew up to cover my ears in a vain attempt to banish the abomination my fingers had created.

Polonaise: so beautiful. How could life be so cruel as to transform something that exquisite, that beloved, into something this ugly and, now from the way it sounded, hated? Where was God? Where was fairness? What had I ever done to deserve such punishment? Why did it have to be my hearing?

I shook a fist at whatever force it was that had robbed me of my music. "It's not fair!" I lamented as, in a moment of supreme frustration, I pounded the same fist so hard against the piano that I thought I had broken a finger. Then I tore the hearing aid off and stuffed it into my pocket.

Seemingly forever, although it might have been only a minute, tears scorched my eyes and burned little rivulets down my cheeks before I sensed, rather than heard, a presence in the room. Oh, great. Was I going to be humiliated on top of everything else? I wanted to vanish.

When I looked up, hoping against hope that it was just Alison, I saw Mark Friedell.

He sat down beside me on the bench and said something I missed. I hated this. I hated starting a conversation with a "What?" Reading Dr. Damon's lips in his office had bolstered my skills with him, but Mark Friedell's were a different set of lips. He even had a mustache, one of my old nemeses.

"I'm sorry," I said.

He looked right at me, and I saw with relief that the mustache didn't completely hide his upper lip. "I haven't seen you for a long time, Abby," he commented as I mentally filled in words I didn't actually see or hear.

I choked back my tears, but he must have seen my distress. He handed me a tissue.

"Thanks," I said, reluctant to meet his eyes. As I tried to pull myself together, what helped was knowing that it was not quite the humiliating moment I had feared it might be. It wasn't Jay Cassidy. It wasn't Kaitlyn Forney, who would have blabbed it all over that deaf Abby was sitting at the piano bawling. This was Mark Friedell, someone I had known since I was five and he was a teenager, and I had begun piano lessons with his grandmother. How long had it been? First he had been away at college and then starting a career as a teacher, and now this was his music room.

"What's wrong?" he asked.

"I . . . I tried playing your piano."

"I can't think of anyone I would rather have play it." Again, he had to repeat, and when I finally understood the sentence, it was bittersweet.

I remembered one afternoon when he had listened to my rendition of *Pathétique* at his grandmother's. He had given me a casual thumbs-up, but I thought I had seen tears in his eyes. What a contrast between then and now!

"You didn't hear me, did you?" I asked with what I felt might be a small voice.

"You mean just now? No."

"Good."

"Why do you say that? Abby, I can't imagine not wanting to hear you play. You have always had a great gift."

"*Had*. That's the word, Mark. It was awful."

He shook his head. "I have trouble believing that. Why do you feel that way?"

"Well, actually, I don't know if my execution was awful or not. It was the sound. The quality."

"What were you playing?"

"Chopin. The way it sounded through my hearing aid," I explained, tapping the little bulge of it in my pocket, "it might as well have been the theme song from some new horror movie." It all gushed out then: the illness, the hearing loss, the sale of my piano.

"This was your first time?"

"Yes, in a long time, and I just wasn't prepared, you know. In the silence of the empty room, I guess I totally forgot my aid was on, and I sat down at the piano on impulse. It's as if I thought it would sound right. I must have Alzheimer's. My playing, radio music, any music at all—it's never sounded right since I was sick. The hearing aid magnifies the sound and manages to twist it—even something beautiful like *Polonaise*—into this horrible, horrible noise. But for a moment I forgot. Dumb me."

"That's heavy, but your talent is intact."

"Is it?"

"I'm willing to bet it is. Why don't you try playing something for me?"

"No way!"

"Okay, but have you thought of just turning your hearing aid off?"

His perception surprised me since everyone else had lambasted me for playing the piano at all, let alone turning off the hearing aid.

"I used to do that before they sold the piano. Most days,

I didn't hear anything at all then when I played."

"Well, that's certainly not ideal, but maybe that's the way you should go, at least with music. Music, after all, is the feeling it engenders, not just the sound, just as fine art is interpretation—an emotional reaction, if you will—as well as paint and canvas."

"You mean, play without sound?" Was he saying that my old way was the right way?

"Yes. You can fill in the blanks with memories of sound and your knowledge of reading music. You are welcome to use this piano whenever the room is free."

I thought about it and agreed on the first part, but there was a problem with his offer to let me play his piano. I was rusty from the lack of practice, and I didn't want anyone coming into the room and hearing me, especially if they compared my current playing to the old me. There wasn't anything "inspired" about it at this point.

And that's how it was decided that instead of playing this piano, I would practice a couple of afternoons a week after school at Mark's house. His grandmother, he explained, had arthritis and had moved to Arizona.

"So, you live in her house now?"

"That's right, and the key is in the same place Grandmother kept it."

I smiled. "No kidding? The geranium pot with the rooster on it?"

"The very one."

Thus began a routine that opened up my life to a joy I had never expected to feel again. I took the hearing aid off at Mark's house and slowly worked my way up through several grade level music books, until finally my fingers no longer felt like leaden balloons.

Although usually I didn't see Mark when I played the piano, now and then our paths crossed at his house, and we talked. I didn't have to summon the word *trust* with Mark. I'd known him for so long that it was just there. He had a natural way of opening me up, especially about school. He even got me started seeing its good aspects, which I certainly had been losing sight of in the wake of my changed comprehension. "Hold those positive things close to you, Abby," Mark advised, "and when the going gets rough, play them back in your mind like a beautiful melody to get you through the day." And that became my armor.

Sharing experiences from his own life to make me feel not so alone in having problems, he told me all kinds of things: about struggling, about freedom of attitude, and life. I saw how people would sometimes do anything to stay alive, to prevail, and for just an instant, I thought I glimpsed a seesaw. At his suggestion, I even talked to one of his teacher friends who was in special ed, and I realized that instead of merely bungling along, I was persevering: I was doing it!

If Mark's essential kindness and empathy, along with my rediscovery that I could still play the piano and enjoy it, empowered me, though, they were also the catalysts of searing self-disappointment and disgust.

It was as if I woke up. How could I have been so stupid as to have fallen for Dr. Damon's "accepted aspect of therapy" line? How naive can a person be? To be sure, I had missed out on lots of girl talk after I got sick, and my mother seemed to think I was twelve instead of sixteen, but how could I have been so blind?

It had to end. I entreated my mother to let me stop seeing Dr. Damon. "He doesn't . . . act right around me, Mom," I began the conversation. I thought I would die bringing it up, but it felt so good to finally tell her that I was ready to spill the whole story. When her reaction stilled my voice, again, I wanted to scream. It was the hearing thing all over again, with my feelings disregarded and my voice unheard. She never even asked me to clarify what I'd meant by his not acting right. Dr. Damon was doing me a world of good, she insisted. I was sometimes coy and acted out, he had told her. *Blah, blah, blah*: my fault, my fault, my fault. Cut to the quick by her dismissal, I never told her.

It wasn't something I wanted to talk about with Dad, and

Paige, who would have listened, was halfway across the country in college. So, I buried it, determined to keep my shame a secret forever.

Since I couldn't get out of going to the sessions, I at least put my foot down, and he and I reached an uneasy stalemate. "Playing hard to get" he called my new determination. My stomach turned over. Well, he could think what he wanted to, but it gave me the creeps to know that he could twist anything around to sound the way he wanted it to: he was, after all, the doctor, and I, just the patient.

He didn't seem to see it, but everything was ruined, including the literary connection I had come to treasure, for I saw clearly how I had let it lead me into something wrong that had far-reaching repercussions. I wasn't the same. Even though he was supportive about school and encouraged me in areas such as seeking higher education, I was left with a swirling potpourri of new, confusing emotions that came to a head gradually and finally bubbled over one day at Mark's.

I was playing *Pathétique*, the piece of music that had years ago brought tears to Mark's eyes at his grandmother's. Somehow, I had to get it just right again. As I played, there was such truth in the beauty of the composition that I thought of Keats and then, because Keats was one of "our" poets, Dr. Damon. Something separated and fell away. Why, Keats was mine! The revelation that trying anything to "keep" literature mine had been for nothing released a floodgate that drenched me in wave after sickening wave of regret. If beauty is truth, then what is ugliness? I had made a terrible connection, given myself away, out of some misguided need to understand, to be understood, and belong. I was no better than a . . . I couldn't put it into words.

Pathetic: that was me.

Emotions roiling, I grabbed the hearing aid from beside the keyboard and reinserted it into my ear. Then I turned the volume up fully and pounded the keys so that the usually haunting strains bombarded my senses and crushed me in raucous noise.

I was so ashamed!

A curtain of tears blinded me to the music on the page, but with a split second of joy, I realized that I remembered all the notes. Then I thought of him and struck the keys with such fury that my hands stung. Notes invaded me like sadistic, smothering spirits, and I gave myself to them completely, until finally they transmogrified back into music.

Then it was over and I was drained.

Just then, Mark's voice boomed. I hadn't seen him walk in, but in the thundering silence after my playing, with my hearing aid still on, I had heard his voice, if not his words. I jumped.

"Mark! How long have you been standing there?" My hand flew up to my ear to flick the switch to OFF.

"Long enough. I have never heard you play with such passion."

He had heard my soul, felt its rent, in my music. I wanted to spill out everything to him, but I knew I shouldn't, so I just busied myself at the piano bench, not wanting him to see my tears. Would he look at me and know? Did it show?

When he sat down beside me, there was that clean, soapy scent of him that I loved so much, but today it just choked me up. What a contrast he was to Dr. Damon's pungent aftershave lotion and sophisticated ways. A sob tore out of me then like some living, breathing beast, startling us both.

"What's wrong, Abby?" I was getting better at reading his lips. Our talks were something I cherished, but today I wasn't happy to see him. Go away, I thought, but he sat there waiting.

I wouldn't look at him, couldn't let him see into me. I would have gotten up to leave, but I felt rooted to the spot.

When I finally spoke, my voice was raspy with emotion. "I can't talk about it."

"Sure you can. What have we been doing these past weeks? I thought we had an open dialogue going." Then he pointed to the customary wooden place on the treble end of the keyboard. "Where's your hearing aid?"

"Here," I said as I angrily pushed back my hair.

"Is it on?"

"It was."

"But you despise the way music sounds with it on."

Amazed by how well he knew me, I nodded again. "That's why I left it on."

"To torture yourself? But why?"

I'm so bad. I'm so awful, my inner voice screamed.

"It's so . . . complicated," I told him.

"Abby, all of it is. What is different about today?" Something in his expression was dangerous because it invited the truth.

"My life is wrecked!"

"Because you can't hear right?" he enunciated clearly.

"No, because of what it's done to me. Because of the way it's robbed me of knowing who I am, of my parents knowing who I am . . . of normality, of fun, of . . . innocence. What am I? Who am I, Mark, but a big set of ears and a forehead with 'Trample me' written all over it? Nobody cares about the real me and my true welfare.

"And what am I to you? Some kind of little experiment? I'm leaving now."

I started to get up, but the gentleness of his hand on my shoulder forced me back down.

"I can't let you leave in this state. Look at me, Abby. You are not—I repeat—you are not 'some kind of little experiment' to me. Please tell me why you are so upset. Is it the music? Living without it?"

"Oh, sure, but that's nothing new. Didn't it ever occur to anybody that I have feelings?"

"You've shared some pretty deep ones with me," he reminded me, referring to tales I had told him about doctors, teachers, and other people, both kind and not. But I hadn't told him this one thing.

I looked right into his eyes. "I don't mean just about hearing aids and stuff. I mean . . . *feelings.*"

"Feelings? Do you mean for guys? They're normal, you

know."

"Tell that to my mom. She thinks I'm still a baby."

"Are you having boyfriend problems?"

I thought of how Jay Cassidy hardly knew I was alive, how Dr. Damon expected me to get in touch with my feelings, and I thought of how much I cared about Mark.

"Mark . . . . "

"Abby, what's going on?"

"I tried to tell my mother."

"And what did she say?"

"She just didn't, well, listen. Feelings, Mark. You know, caring, trusting, admiring. If it was anybody, it should have been someone like you."

He looked concerned. "What is it you tried to tell your mother?"

Unbidden, I remembered his touch with revulsion, but he had offered me hope and options where I had felt none, and I had been so afraid of losing myself again that I had been willing to do anything.

I started shaking.

Like the caring person Mark was, he reached out for me and just held me gently as I sobbed into his chest. I had a new knowledge of relationships: of touch, of smell, and especially, of right and wrong.

And as alone as I felt, it didn't feel right to tell Mark.

⟿Chapter Thirteen⟿

In light of the bombshell that Kelly Graham dropped, it's unsettling to think that I almost didn't meet with her. Kelly Graham? The name had rung no bells, but when it turned up prominently, with a blue asterisk beside it, in Abby's purse-sized address book, I called her without hesitation.

Kelly's eagerness intrigued me. Why didn't I come over? she suggested. Even so, would one more interview help? Images from talks with others swirled in my mind to the extent that, as dearly as I still wanted to find answers, I didn't know if I had room to incorporate anything new.

In the end, what made me go was Kelly's comment that Abby had come to her for insight into parenting a deaf child. What had Abby learned, if anything, from this woman, and hadn't I also wanted to understand my parents? Maybe in addition to learning something new about Abby, this time I would also chance upon something else.

I could see immediately why Abby would have liked Kelly, as she exuded a vivaciousness that even her obvious deep regret and lingering shock about Abby couldn't mask. Her incredible aquamarine eyes, which might have seemed glacial, had a sparkle that invited me in.

"Abby was very special to me and my son, Jared," she reiterated after we had introduced ourselves and she had told me how sorry she was. We sat in a small living room made cheerful by splashes of sunny yellow upholstery.

"How did you meet?"

"By chance. Abby, apparently wanting to understand your parents, asked a teacher to direct her to someone with a deaf child. That someone turned out to be me."

Wanted to understand them . . . .

I remembered how I had sometimes felt cast by the wayside by my parents after my sister's illness, including after her death. It occurred to me that, perhaps in a different way, they had closed themselves off to Abby. Had it been only my perception that they had done everything so right with her? What had Abby been feeling? I was glad now that I had come to talk to Kelly Graham.

Before we had time to get into anything, a towheaded boy of about six bounded into the room. Kelly moved her hands, and his smaller ones flitted like canaries. His facial expressions and body language changed along with the movement of his hands, and it was fascinating to watch what looked like such a complete, yet wordless, exchange.

"This is Jared," Kelly introduced. "I told him that you are Abby's sister. He adored her and asked where she was. I explained before and just reminded him."

I nodded, sobered to think of their friend who would never be back. Then I focused back upon the beautiful child, who moved closer to us.

"Hi, Jared. I'm sorry that I don't know how to sign. Would you tell me your name in sign language?"

After his mother interpreted, he outlined the letter J in the air with his little finger up near his hair.

"That's his name sign," Kelly explained.

I smiled at him and then noticed that he was holding a sheet of paper. I copied the name sign and said, "That's the most wonderful dinosaur I have ever seen. May I look at it more closely?"

Responding to my outstretched hand, rather than my words, he gave it to me rather shyly, but I could tell from the emergent little grin that he was pleased. Then his fingers started flying again.

"What's he saying?" I asked Kelly.

"He wants you to know that dinosaurs lived a long time ago and are now extinct. His favorite is the T-Rex. He likes to mottle the colors like that and is very proud when he uses every shade in the box."

"Which is your favorite?" I asked, looking at Kelly.

"Talk to Jared, not to me," she gently advised.

I wasn't accustomed to being around anyone who signed, but I should have known better. Abby, too, had appreciated eye contact and direct communication. The memory of her asking a saleswoman at the mall to repeat something sprang to mind. Disregarding Abby in a way that seemed to say she wasn't worth the effort, the woman had turned to me and said something like, "Tell her I need an extra five dollars. The sale price doesn't apply to this item." Abby had picked right up on the dismissal, and I had watched as a little something flickered out inside of her, just as surely as a light. So, I regretted my lapse with Jared.

"Oh, I'm sorry."

There was no reprimand in Kelly's voice, though. "Don't be. It's just that I've seen so many older deaf people get cut off when others talk as though they aren't really there. I've gotten defensive. I don't want that happening to Jared, especially not at home. It's a little confusing, I know, when you are first around signers."

I might have told her about Abby and the mall, but Kelly was busily interpreting something to her son, and I remembered my question about the color. In reply, Jared's index finger zeroed in on a green spot on the dinosaur's head.

"The color of money," Kelly laughed.

I smiled, glad that we had gotten past the communication glitch. "Jared," I said, looking directly at him, "I think green is cool, too, like the grass and leaves. It even matches your shirt."

When his mother conveyed my words, he seemed to realize the match for the first time and took a delight in it, pointing from the shirt to the green in the dinosaur and back again.

Then he got into another discussion with his mother, and my mind wandered. How often had Abby been cut off? I remembered holiday dinners with lots of family, which meant people talking at different points around the dining room table, and Abby sitting there, forgotten, until someone remembered that she wasn't hearing and wasn't necessarily included. How often had Aunt Carol or someone else suddenly remembered, only to spoil it, saleswoman fashion, with something such as, "Does Abby want the pumpkin pie or the mince?" shutting her out of direct communication. And that was family!

How many times, in how many different settings, had that happened? Jared was fortunate to have a mother tuned in to his needs, and except for not hearing, he seemed, right down to the two missing front teeth, like any other exuberant six-year-old, proud of his artwork and eager to learn.

Jared's wave brought me out of my thoughts.

"He's going to watch Bert and Ernie now," Kelly informed me.

"'Bye, Jared. It was nice to meet you."

There was another short, animated spurt of conversation between the mother and her son. "He wants you to have his dinosaur."

"Oh, what a wonderful gift. Thank you, Jared. I am going to put it on my refrigerator. My mother used to do that with my pictures from school."

Jared smiled broadly when his mother explained, and then he was gone.

"Was he born deaf?" I asked, very interested in learning all about him.

Kelly related how she had had cytomegalovirus when she was pregnant with Jared. He was an alert, bright baby, but they had begun suspecting that everything wasn't right when he reached his first birthday and had not said any first words, not even *ma ma* and those other precursors to spoken language. Friends and even her doctor hadn't thought it was that unusual and weren't concerned, but it kept nagging at Kelly, who thought it prudent to have Jared's hearing tested.

"It was just a mother's instinct and observation, and that's when we knew."

I thought of my parents during and right after Abby's illness. It was if the life had been whooshed out of them. "It must have been a blow."

"Even though we had suspected hearing loss, it was, Paige; it was devastating. My husband, Don, and I actually went through an emotional interlude parallel to the grief process, a letting go, I guess, of the illusion of the perfect child. You have all these hopes and dreams when you carry a child and give birth and see that wondrous little human masterpiece for the first time, and our finding out shattered our idea of what Jared was and would become. We were filled with an amazing host of emotions, especially fear."

I nodded, thinking of the near-terror in my parents' eyes when Abby had awakened from the coma and not heard right. "Fear: my parents had that, too. Can you explain it, Kelly? Is it possible to put something like that into words?"

"Abby and I talked about that same thing. It was, like, you know: What's going to happen to Jared? What do deaf people do with their lives? Will he ever be happy and well adjusted? Will he learn? Will he talk? How will other people perceive him? This list went on and on, and we felt sick as we contemplated the possible ramifications. In my case, I also felt guilty because I was the one who had carried the virus."

"How did Abby relate to that?"

"It seemed to be a revelation to her, and she said that kind of fear was something she, herself, lived with."

"Do you think she and my parents talked about their mutual fears and other feelings?"

Kelly shook her head sadly. "No. I think they may have thought that by verbalizing them, they would come true. I don't know for sure."

Fear and other emotions not being verbalized: I would think more about that later. "So, what happened with Jared? How did you proceed?"

"A little time passed, and we realized that we needed answers to our questions, so we took our pediatrician's advice and began taking Jared to a clinic specializing in infant hearing loss."

"And did that help?"

"Oh, enormously, but I'll have to admit that it didn't happen overnight. We clung to our idea of the 'perfect' child, so for a long while, we concentrated upon looking for some magic potion to make him hear right. Toward this end, we tried or considered all kinds of things to foster our idea of normality: hearing aids, drugs, diet, faith healers, and cochlear implants. Are you familiar with cochlear implants?"

I nodded, thinking of the electronic device that some- how bypasses the damaged parts of the ear, connects the nerve fibers, and sends coded sound signals to the brain. "My parents were considering an implant for Abby."

"I know. She mentioned it. Did you know that she had very serious reservations about that?"

"No. Why wouldn't she have wanted one? I mean, she was so normal before she got sick, so why wouldn't she do any- thing in her power to hear better, especially since the hearing aid wasn't working very well for her?"

"There you go. That 'normal' business is what kept us hamstrung with Jared at first. Don't get me wrong. By no means am I against implants. In fact, I met a twelve-year-old girl who is doing beautifully with one—cochlear implants seem to be the wave of the future—but they aren't for everyone, either, Paige."

"You mean they don't work?"

"I'm hardly an expert on this, but in Abby's case, just think of it. At best, the implant would only have made her hard of hearing. She was a musician who was accustomed to entirely normal sound. What it comes down to is that she was terrified of getting stuck with what she called `synthesized noise' that would neither bring back full-bodied, beautiful sounds like her music nor necessarily let her distinguish speech. Worse, she wouldn't have been able to take the implant out at will as she took the hearing aid off. She wasn't dead-set against it, but she didn't want to jump into something like that, and that's why she was leaning more toward developing her speechreading. She wanted to give that a good try, and it seemed to be working for her when she turned off the hearing aid and fully utilized her visual perception and her knowledge of the English language."

Quality of sound was something Dr. Black had mentioned, so I saw more than ever that it must be far more important than those of us who heard normally imagined. The rapture on Abby's face when she played the piano, after all, had been, to what degree I couldn't know, in the exquisiteness of the sound. What would it have been like to have moved her fingers across the keys in the old, familiar way, only to produce something of greatly diminished quality? It was just so much more complex than I had allowed myself to imagine.

"Are you saying that Abby was all right the way she was? What if the implant had brought it all back and made her normal?" She hadn't been all right, and she obviously hadn't felt normal, or she wouldn't be gone. A current of anger at Kelly shot through me.

"Wasn't she normal? Or was it that others didn't believe that she was?"

"Do you think of Jared as normal?"

"Of course! Even though he's profoundly deaf, he's normal."

"How did you let go of the idea of the 'perfect' child and come to this conclusion?"

"Well, after Jared was diagnosed, we tried hearing aids without any real response. We met other parents, deaf adults, and professionals at a support group at the infant hearing loss clinic, and we eventually realized that Jared was not going to be as limited as we had feared. We even began to feel very fortunate when we met parents of children with multiple disabilities that included blindness and severe neurological complications beyond the deafness.

"It was recommended that we use signs with him, so we took classes in American Sign Language and started signing with Jared soon afterwards. It was just like watching a flower open, Paige, in the way a child's world expands when he hears words and understands them and you understand when he says them back to you. It was true communication," she said as her voice cracked with emotion at the memory of breaking through the understanding barrier with Jared, "and it struck us that it didn't matter that it was visual instead of auditory. Jared was Jared, the same, beautiful, whole person he had been from the start, and we began thinking positively about what he could do, instead of about what he might never accomplish. We looked for the right school, the right modifications to his life. To paraphrase I. King Jordan, the president of Gallaudet University for the deaf, Jared can do anything but hear.

"As for the cochlear implant, we don't want our son to feel there is anything wrong with being deaf. It's still an option, but it's one about which we want Jared to have a say-so."

To what extent my parents had included Abby in decision-making I didn't know, and might never know, but I liked Kelly's attitude and hoped Abby's viewpoints and wishes had carried weight with those who mattered. It occurred to me that maybe she hadn't been listened to, and perhaps that, at least in part, explained the hauntedness in my parents' eyes that somehow went beyond my sister's death. Maybe they hadn't done everything as perfectly as it seemed.

Dr. Black had said that perhaps Abby should have been where she was educationally, and perhaps not, but after having spoken with his wife, I thought she had been in the right place, in public school.

It was probably self-evident, but I asked anyway. "Is Jared in special education classes?"

"He attends the school for the deaf. All the classes are special there. He's fine with it, and we are, too. He's learning, he has friends, and he has teachers who, for the most part, understand his limitations and respect his potentialities. But, remember, he never had a normal language base, as your sister did; that greatly influences the right educational setting, and I got the feeling that Abby was in the right place for her."

"That's what I think. Someone else told me that it isn't as simple as just learning sign language. Abby loved the English language."

"Her knowledge and memory of it—the syntax, morphology, and the whole gamut of the thing we call language—made public school and speechreading viable options for her. She was doing a slam-bang job of it, too. It really amazed me. She made mistakes in comprehension here and there, especially if I abruptly changed the subject, and there were some gaps in what she saw on people's lips, but it seemed quite adequate. She was learning to make it do. Her memories of sound, and not just spoken sound, were very important to her."

Something dawned on me then. Perhaps for a person like Abby, so steeped in spoken language and music, remembered sound was enough and somehow better than a flooding with—what had Kelly said Abby called it?—"synthesized noise."

"Do you feel that the hearing aid was a mistake?" I asked.

"It's not how I feel here that counts, Paige. It's how Abby felt and Jared feels."

I sighed, and when I spoke again, it was very softly. "I wonder if I ever really knew Abby."

"I'm sure you did, but maybe you didn't know this new side of her in relation to her total being."

I came out of myself then and grasped something. Had anybody? There, perhaps, lay the cornerstone for Abby's death: In making that one facet of her, her hearing loss, so important, and ironically in trying to do so much for her, we had all too often neglected to remember a uniqueness that included Abby's hopes, fears, dreams, innate ability . . . her normality. As Kelly had in the beginning with Jared, we had assumed that Abby could no longer do this, that she needed that, and sometimes we had spent so much time feeling sorry for her, or were into her physical condition, that we lost sight of the fact that she was still just . . . just Abby.

A giant's hand squeezed my heart and I squinched my eyes shut as my heart's blood seemed to pool in them. Through the red haze, I saw Abby running from the crab, Abby parroting me, Abby winning her first blue ribbon as a budding pianist,

Abby making little presents for elderly neighbors. I saw that in the daze of sudden deafness, that little girl had still been there, that same unique person, only like a veneer, we had let the hearing loss obscure the substance.

Finally, I opened my eyes and looked at Kelly. Her gentle nod allowed my tears to spill over as they never had.

Kelly handed me a tissue when they were spent and I looked up again. "Do you want to talk about it?" she invited.

"Thanks. I'm not sure I can put it into words. We all just made so many mistakes, Kelly."

"I understand. I made them, too, with Jared. Paige, it won't do any good to blame yourself."

"Or my parents, I guess. It was something you said about wanting Jared to have a say-so and not wanting him to feel there was anything wrong with being deaf. My parents, I thought, were always acting in my sister's best interest, but to what extent had they ripped away Abby's self-esteem and her right to have some say in decisions that affected her life so pervasively? I don't blame them as much as I feel for Abby, trapped by other people's expectations, hopes, fears, and dreams . . . and some ridiculous quest to keep her normal when she never stopped being that way at all. A part of me resents them for that, Kelly, for not achieving what you did in your attitude toward Jared's loss of hearing, and yet another part of me feels for them on a new level because I suddenly understand what's been going on with them. A grief process, you called it.

"In a way, we all killed Abby with our deficient attitudes, well-intentioned 'help,' in not really listening to her, by taking freedoms from her, and by making her feel invisible, isolated, and devalued. I'm just as much to blame as anyone else.

"But do you know what really killed her, Kelly? Deafness killed my sister!"

Kelly reacted by shaking her head emphatically. "No, it didn't! You put your finger on some of it, Paige, but deafness is only a condition, a state of being. It was the handling of the situation that arose from that condition that complicated Abby's life, but it goes a lot further."

"I'm not following."

"You'll have to admit, for one thing, that the pregnancy had an enormous impact upon her."

At first I thought I hadn't heard Kelly Graham correctly. Why would someone's pregnancy have much of an effect upon Abby? Then I sucked in my breath, remembering how I had so recently plumped my mother's pillows and how fragile she had looked in bed or sitting in the wing chair. No wonder Dad had whisked her off to Greece. My mother was pregnant! There's no doubt that that would have affected Abby, who had always been "the baby" of the family. It certainly floored me.

"My mother?"

Kelly just stared at me, aquamarine eyes filled with some strange something that I couldn't quite define.

"Kelly?"

"I'm so sorry. I thought you knew. It's not your mother, Paige. Abby was expecting a child."

I couldn't breathe. In fact, I was sure I was going to pass out. I had to have heard wrong. "Excuse me."

"I'm afraid you heard me correctly. She was pregnant. She confided it to me."

But not to me. Had my parents known? Did that explain some of their grief and their inability to talk to me about my sister? Were they protecting me? Abby? Themselves? No, there had to be some mistake.

"She didn't even have a boyfriend."

"I don't know about that."

"But you heard it from Abby's own lips that she was pregnant?" It seemed incredible not only that my sister might have been carrying a new life but that this woman whom I'd never heard of until a few days ago had known this momentous thing about my sister while I had not.

"Yes," she said.

"Did my parents know?"

"I don't think so. I encouraged her to tell them. She said

that Mark wanted her to, as well."

"Mark?" If it was possible, it had just gotten even worse.

"That teacher she was seeing."

I felt the color drain from my face. "Seeing?" I left the question hanging. Certainly Kelly wasn't implying that he was the father.

She was looking at the floor.

"There's something you're not saying, Kelly. I need to know. I'm going crazy here, trying to understand why my sister would have disregarded her principles, first by getting pregnant and then by killing herself. It just isn't the Abby I knew or, I guess, thought I knew. What do you know? What is it you aren't telling me?"

She continued looking at the carpet for long moments before finally meeting my eyes. "I never planned to say this to anyone but Don, who pointed out that I have absolutely nothing to substantiate it. I don't know if it will help or just make everything worse, but, Paige, I don't think Abby killed herself."

Incredulous, I just stared at her.

"Are you all right?" she asked.

"All right? Boy, I don't know. At first, I didn't think she killed herself, either. I still don't want to believe it, but, Kelly, it's the only thing it could have been."

She shook her head. "There's one other possibility."

"You can't mean—"

"I do. Someone killed Abby."

─Chapter Fourteen─

Abby

"Feelings" Journal:
It can't be! Could I be that unlucky just when the
fates seemed to be smiling down on me? The sun
is shining, the sky is still blue, so everything will be
all right with me, won't it? Don't let it be what I think
it is . . . .

When the little kit I bought in a drugstore when I was sure nobody was looking confirmed my worst suspicion, I was stunned out of my mind. Pregnant! Me? Enveloped in a fog of disbelief, I sleepwalked through my daily routine. When I came to, I alternated between panic that turned my hands icy and thinking it might just go away. When it didn't, I plunged head-long into a crevasse of despair. Then it was like being on a seesaw gone amok as I began agonizing over the most crucial decision of my life. There's just no describing the terror tinged by some new, misty sense of something wondrous happening.

It's amazing how one right choice can set a person free. As the weeks passed and I told no one and did nothing, I had made my decision, springing myself from a trap that maybe I had been in from the moment I had come out of my coma after meningitis. Now, suddenly, I was in control . . . sort of. The panic didn't suddenly disappear, but a new determination strengthened me, and I began to look inward.

Mark noted a change in me, but if he had wondered before, he couldn't have missed it when I broached a topic that broke my heart. "I think I'm going to have to stop coming here, Mark," I said.

"But you love playing my piano."

I smiled, but that outward sign of agreement quickly melted into the depths of me, where a new reality colored my world. I couldn't have people insinuating awful things about Mark and me. "I do, but it's better that I don't come for awhile."

"Tell me why." The gentleness in his expression let me know he had spoken softly, but there was something in his dark eyes—something imploring—that made me realize he deserved the truth.

It came out matter-of-factly, and from the way he had inhaled sharply, I knew it was the last thing he had expected me to reveal.

"You're the only person other than a doctor at a women's clinic who knows. Promise me you won't tell anyone," I admonished after he had begun to digest the news. He looked concerned, but I noticed with relief, not judgmental.

"And you haven't told your parents?" he asked.

I shook my head. "I can't."

"Abby, it may seem that way, but . . . . "

I was glad he had paused. I didn't need a lecture. "It's not as simple as you might think."

"I'm sorry if I made it sound that way. I know it's very complicated."

"Mark, you have to keep your promise."

"Not to tell them? I will for now, but they are going to find out in time, you know."

I nodded.

"Then why wait? They could be of tremendous support to you. You shouldn't have to deal with something of this magnitude alone."

"I'm waiting because . . . because—oh, you wouldn't understand."

"Try me."

The way he had spoken as an invitation, rather than a challenge or a demand, made me want to share it with him. "They'd make me get rid of it. Mark, it would be just like the hearing aid. They would make the decision. They would drag me to the doctor's. It would be about them, or maybe me to the extent that they think they know me, but certainly not about the baby. And it's the baby I have to think about, to protect. I just feel very strongly about that."

"Your welfare is also important. It's not easy to raise a child and be a single parent. It's challenging enough for anyone, but you are only sixteen."

I laughed mirthlessly. "Don't you think I know that? I don't have any illusions about having a cute little baby to love and love me back. I know it's not all frilly bonnets or tiny suits with sailboats on them. Motherhood is a serious commitment, and I know I'm not ready for that kind of responsibility."

"You would give it up for adoption? That's not easy, either."

"Are you trying to play devil's advocate?"

"No. I'm just taking a look at the situation and exploring the options. If you were my sister, I would want to spare you any emotional pain that I could. I would also probably want to deck the guy who did this to you."

Mark's words made my thoughts drift to *him*. "I didn't ask for this. I didn't want it to happen. It has, though, and I just have to do what's right. Keeping this secret until it's too late for my parents to force me into anything is right. Besides, I'm not blameless. I should have known what was happening."

Mark clenched his fists. "Who is he, Abby?"

Right then, I wished the tiny life inside me, if it had to be there at all, were Mark's. Whatever his emotions about this were—anger, pity, disappointment, or something else—he cared. He was on my side. I knew that he was someone I could have loved, someone worthy of all the love in the world, and it just cut me up inside again that I had let myself be led into the kind of loveless dependence that had gotten me into this sorry situation. What if I told Mark that my psychiatrist had gotten me pregnant? No, it was better that he think it was some guy from school. How many people got pregnant because they didn't want to give up literary discussions, anyway? How stupid can a woman be? *Woman?* That was a laugh, for lately even with the tiny life growing inside of me, or maybe because of it, I realized how young I was, and I wanted nothing more than to be a carefree *girl*.

"Someone I don't think you know," I said.

"Does he know?"

"No."

"Are you planning to tell him?"

"No."

"Your saying you don't think you should come here any-more: that was to protect me, wasn't it?"

I looked away, suddenly shy around him. He was the one who finally broke the silence.

"Okay. I really appreciate that, but you were coming here regularly when it must have happened, so I think you should be here now whenever you want to be. I have the feeling that Grandmother's piano may be even more important to you now."

And it was. I played . . . and I thought . . . and I played . . . and I thought . . . .

Maybe it was because of the way the music soothed me that I began considering the timeless values of human existence, such as the way we all need to love and be loved. I didn't know why, but the word *Camiros* crept into my thoughts, teasing me to remember what it was and where I had heard it.   I never did recall exactly where, but when I remembered that it was a place, it all started coming together. It was at Camiros, a long-dead town in Greece—one of the towns supposedly built by the mythical grandsons of Apollo—that an ancient inscription still reportedly exists among the timeworn ruins of an apricot-hued temple. *Xaîpe*: "Be happy" is all it says, yet in a way, it says it all. What had the Greeks been thinking when they chiseled it into stone more than two thousand years ago? Was it a farewell to the dead? Advice to the living? The simple directive was, when I thought about it, not so simple at all. Like a tantalizing riddle, the Ancients, perhaps on purpose, had left it for each person to discern how to be happy.

True values, feelings, happiness . . . what had been fomenting in the back of my mind suddenly broke free and soared into my consciousness as dramatically as a butterfly emerging from a cocoon and taking flight.

Connections: it was all about connections, I saw now. I had *re*connected with something vital within myself, and whether it was my own humanity or something else I wasn't sure, but whatever I called it, it gave me a sense of purpose and hope. I wasn't a grain of sand, forgotten, unimportant, and spiritless. It was not for me to let others lead me along, knowingly or unknowingly guiding me into actions that might satisfy them or connect them to me in their minds but sever me from myself if I followed.

Be happy. As I touched the piano, the result was silence, but music was part of my happiness, part of that connection that gave meaning to my life. In one shining instant, elation shot through me as I realized that music was mine forever, for its beauty was embedded within my soul so that no one could take it from me, ever, even if I were consigned to the physical reality of distorted sound or total silence, and even if I were deprived of a piano.

I heard it in my mind, and not just sketchily but in all its full-bodied depth. It, as well as entire symphonies, was mine—all mine in a totality of remembered glory.

I smiled. I was whole again. Had I ever stopped being so? Maybe, or maybe not, but I knew that I couldn't, wouldn't, let anyone reduce me into being just "the deaf girl" or someone who needed to be repaired. I was a deaf girl, to be sure, but I was so much more. And I was fine—I was actually fine!—just the way I was, mangled hearing included.

With that came the realization that one of life's most important gifts, if not the most vital, is freedom of attitude. I had a choice about my hearing, too, for I could let myself be crushed or I could endure and become stronger and better in the process.

As life went from black-and-white into full color, I was spurred by burgeoning feelings of self-discovery into action. Instead of trying to shut out memories of sound or mourn the absence of particular sounds, for instance, I embraced them fully, remembering them in a way that, in turn, elicited life-affirming recollections that had been dying because I had allowed other people's attitudes to skew my perceptions.

Memories of sound both profound and simple flooded me. Take the everyday sound of an electric mixer, for example. In my memory bank, that certain, wonderful hum is synonymous with a grandmother in a checked apron beating frosting for her secret-recipe black walnut cake. How extraordinary it seemed that the thought of that distinctive whir had the power to bring back the image of powdered sugar on her forearms, the scent of vanilla combined with her light floral cologne, and the resonance of her humming some old song. She had taught me the words to many of her old favorites, and sometimes we had broken into something like *With a Song in My Heart* at the drop of a hat as her sturdy fingers spread icing on the cake and I dropped on walnut halves.

In shutting out the memory of that whir—the trigger to a particular memory—I had lost a little piece of Grandma and a slice of my history. Now, I had found that part of her, as well as facets of countless other people, by opening myself to remembered sounds.

I drew them in to me, enveloped myself in their uniqueness so as never to forget, and there was comfort and healing. That way of thinking expanded my horizons, not only giving me back birdsong and music without guilt for "living in the past" or sadness for what had been and now was not, but propelling me toward a letting go, an acceptance of who I was. I saw so clearly that it was not the "what" that mattered; it was the "who," the inner me. I sensed that perhaps for always there would be down times, such as Christmas when the carols I'd so loved played, when I missed real, normal hearing in the here and now, but to balance that ache, I focused upon the perceptions I was gleaning.

This is not to say that people who are born deaf and who don't have "sound banks" can't be happy, too; they define their own happiness, which is as right and valid for them as mine is for me.

My change of attitude had a ripple effect. Once I had decided that remembering sounds to the utmost of my capacity was a good thing, and not the detriment that many people had implied, I noticed a sharpening of my ability to read lips in almost any setting, for every speaker suddenly, almost as if by magic, had a voice that I imagined, complete with pitch and inflections. It was the linchpin that transformed reading lips into something far more personalized and connecting than it had ever been. Instead of simply watching mouths flap ever so silently or straining for well-formed words that had no sound, I "heard" voices almost uncannily. It's probably not surprising that my lipreading skill improved by leaps and bounds, until I was reading lips far more than struggling to get speech over a little grunt here and a big sneeze there through my hearing aid. I just left it off, without guilt.

My grandmother used to say that life is like a glass of water. I now saw what she meant. State of mind: it was all about attitude, and about prevailing over those who hurt you, those who don't understand, and maybe most of all, over your own doubts, insecurities, fears, and shortcomings.

Mark had continued her half-empty, half-full philosophy by advising me to concentrate upon the positive, so as I had done in school at his suggestion, I now looked for what was right with the world, and I found it all around me. A sunset clarified it for me. I first noticed it as a glaring nuisance. Then I looked again and saw the exquisite tangerine orb staining the sky flame color and rose. A big, fat cumulus cloud rimmed with gold sent a current of pleasure through me so that I detected something larger and more relevant than my own situation. I realized then that as long as the sun still set every evening and rose the next morning, there was hope.

It was there in the beauty of nature: in the sunset, in the

lone wildflower growing defiantly through a crack in the sidewalk, and in the precision of a robin feeding her young after having returned to the right nesting climate in the spring.

I saw it when I looked at people, as well: something as simple as a mother blowing bubbles with her toddler, or a woman holding open a door for an octogenarian. Perhaps even more, I saw it in the way human beings handle adversity. Hadn't Mark been trying to tell me that suffering is relative? A minor hurdle for one person could be an insurmountable obstacle to another, but that didn't diminish the first person's struggle, for we all approach each new instance of anguish, each new trial, as novices. Who is to say which is more profound: the grief of a mother who has lost a baby who will never have a first birthday, a first day of school, and so many life experiences; or the grief of a mother who has lost a grown child whose promise has been fulfilled but who must now unmesh from that child's long presence in her life?

Compassion and not judging others . . . . My attitude toward my parents also began to change. I thought of Kelly Graham, whose perceptions as the mother of a deaf boy helped me understand where they were coming from. Although probably it shouldn't have surprised me, I was taken aback to realize from Kelly that my parents, as well as I, had been adjusting to the far-reaching changes brought on by my illness and resultant deafness. A grief process she had called it. "I'm not taking sides," she had said, "but their hearts broke for you, Abby, and may be continuing to break." Maybe, then, they just hadn't moved on yet, and I determined right then to help them by learning more about this process. Whatever I could do to help them accept my hearing loss I would, reassuring them about my potentialities and my place in the world.

I became more resilient in school. Oh, it was still a struggle, but things that used to bother me didn't as much now. A case in point is when one teacher noticed me laughing heartily with the rest of the class and somehow guessed that I hadn't actually followed the train of discussion. "What are you laughing about, Abby?" he had asked. It's funny. Whereas before I would have withered into my shoes to be singled out that way, I stopped to consider the question with an open mind and found that it wasn't so bad. I was laughing, I saw, not to fool people, not to be like everyone else, but because I had felt their pleasure, which had struck some chord within me. "I'm laughing," I told him, "because everyone else is." He had pondered my reply and decided that that was the essence of a laugh.

More secure with myself, and with the eventual goal of college in mind, it was also easier to stand up for myself and to ask for help when I needed it; we are all marbled with both strengths and limitations, after all. If a teacher actually belittled me, I was less likely than before to internalize it, since I knew it was essentially her problem, not mine. My responsibility was to rise above it by persevering. *I* was that little guy in the open boat on the rough seas, and it was up to me to keep rowing. In doing so, I even began to find a certain richness within myself.

Be happy. My purpose, as I saw it, was to help myself so that I could ultimately help other people. I knew that started with taking care of myself and then finding the courage to give my baby the gift of parents wiser and more prepared than I. I wasn't yet sure how I would realize my happiness in the long run, but I had taken the first important steps in that direction.

Be happy . . . but not at another's expense. I couldn't let anyone walk all over me. Dr. Damon had exploited my vulnerability to foster his own need for power and control, or whatever it was that defined his happiness. It just couldn't go on or extend to cast a shadow over still another life.

Out of a sense of humanity, rather than revenge, I knew it was up to me to blow the whistle on him.

~Chapter Fifteen~

My talk with Kelly Graham left me reeling. Abby pregnant?

I want my wedding day to be perfect, my pony-tailed sister had asserted not long before her illness, and I knew from the tenor of the conversation that she was talking about more than the big white wedding of her dreams; she meant waiting for the right guy and the right time. Why, she had been as adamant about that as . . . .

Never in a million years, her voice came out of nowhere vowing never to take her own life.

Pregnancy. Suicide. But murder?

No, as much as I wanted to believe that my little sister hadn't taken her own life—and I had been over it dozens of times in my ruminations, trying to find an escape hatch—murder just didn't make sense. There had been an autopsy. Certainly a crime of that magnitude would have been detected, and who would have taken the life, anyway, of such a mild sweet teenager? With nothing to substantiate her suspicion, what it boiled down to was simply that Kelly, too, must have a desperate longing to find some answer other than self-destruction.

Murder discounted, that still left me wrestling with pregnancy and suicide.

Why, Abby? Didn't I know you at all? What happened, exactly, to make you violate not only one, but two, such fervently held personal codes of conduct?

A memory flashed into focus: me as a young teenager and Abby at around seven years of age. A bad hair day had led me to try to disguise myself with a kerchief hiding my unruly mane. Sunglasses furthered what I hoped was a disappearing act. Mom had insisted that I walk to the mini-mart for something, and Abby, as she so often did, wanted to tag along. I'll never forget her kerchief and sunglasses, and her aping my every mannerism that afternoon. Of course, instead of blending into the sidewalks and the aisles of merchandise, I had stood out like a sore thumb, thanks to my cute little sister's antics.

My heart broke all over again. A perfect wedding day ruined . . . suicide . . . and I knew I would give anything, just anything, to be as irritated with Abby as I had been that afternoon when she was only seven.

I had known her so well then, but it was as if that awful illness had sent us spinning away from each other, and where had my questioning gotten me? Had I found her or lost even more of her?

I wondered if my parents had known at the end that she was pregnant, or if they had discovered it only after the fact, through the postmortem. Which would have been worse: to have known one's daughter was expecting a child and have her die, or not to have guessed, only to find out after her sudden death? The memory of Dad's heated exchange with Jay Cassidy's father sprang to mind. Of course! Now I understood. The whole family had known about Abby's feelings for Jay, so it seemed natural that he be suspected as the father. Had he been? Had my parents known? Maybe it made no difference now. Whoever it had been, and at whatever point in time my parents had discovered my sister's pregnancy, how shocked they would have been. I would have shut down, too. They deserved their healing vacation in Greece.

At the same time, another part of me was furious with them. How could they not have known? How could a mother, especially, not see it in her daughter? Had they been so wrapped up in their crusade to save my sister's hearing that they had been oblivious to almost everything else? Had they even seen that she had turned from a child into an appealing young woman?

And where did Mark Friedell fit into this? What was it Kelly had said? That Abby had told her Mark wanted her to tell my parents? So, he had known! After all the time we had spent together, and especially in light of the emotions we had shared about Abby, not to mention our growing affection for each other, that he hadn't said a word to me about something as significant as my sister's pregnancy made me sick. Why? Was my trust in him misplaced? Was the Mark Friedell I thought I knew only an illusion?

Shaking my head, I couldn't help remembering our last time together, just two days before Kelly's startling revelations. Mark had been preparing to leave on a short trip to Arizona to celebrate his grandmother's birthday, he had told me with both anticipation and regret in his voice.

"You will be her best present," I said. The words were barely out of my mouth when he held out a small gift-wrapped package. Mustache and all, he looked like a very pleased little boy right then, and I felt my heart turn over to think how precious he was fast becoming to me. "What's this?"

"It's for you."

"But it's not my birthday or anything."

"I know, but when I saw this in a store, I just had to buy it for you."

I shook the package. "What is it?"

"Open it and find out," he laughed.

"Duh. This is just so unexpected," I said as I pulled away the ribbon and undid the mauve foil paper. Fingers clumsy with surprise and anticipation, I opened, first, the cardboard jeweler's box, and then, nestled inside, another, brown velvet box. I pried open the hinged lid.

"Oh, Mark!"

"Do you know what it symbolizes?"

It was a gold charm in the shape of a little girl, and there was just one thing engraved across the bodice of her dress: the letter *X*. Recalling Mark's emotion when he had related his memory of seeing the child's brown wool dress at Mauthausen, I was touched beyond words. When I spoke, my voice was husky with feeling. "It's the little girl . . . . "

He nodded. "When you understood and we talked about the importance of never forgetting, I think I started to fall in love with you right then and there, Paige. Put it on the bracelet you plan to start."

In love . . . . My smile wafted to my lips from the orchestra pit in my heart. It was true: the thousand violins that I had laughed to hear other people talk about actually played!

Looking back, it was strange that when I finally found some words, I asked, "The bracelet? How did you know I was thinking about starting one?"

"From Abby. She was thinking ahead to your birthday and mentioned that she had been looking for the perfect charm for a perfect sister. She told me that you had admired an aunt's bracelet and had always wanted to start one for yourself."

Mark's sensitivity, my sister's perception, and her mention of "the perfect charm for a perfect sister" stirred me deeply, and through soft tears, I said, "I think this is the most wonderful gift anyone has ever give me, Mark. Thank you from the bottom of my heart. I will treasure it always, and I will start that bracelet."

Then he kissed me, long and tenderly, and I knew that we had entered a new dimension of our relationship.

"I love you, too," I whispered.

Now, sick at heart, I fingered the little-girl charm, which was temporarily on a chain around my neck. Why hadn't he told me my sister was expecting a child?

I had to know. I dialed his phone number: "You have reached 555-1476. I can't come to the phone right now, but . . . . "

Dispirited, I hung up. Stupid me. He wasn't back from Green Valley yet. His plane was due in soon, though, and I knew what I had to do.

As I paced around Mark's small living room after having let myself in with the key in the rooster pot, impatient to find out why he had known about my sister and I had not, I felt my heart turn over. The room had become so . . . Mark: the piano, of course; built-in bookcases chock-full of a wonderful medley of classics, popular novels, European history tomes, and the black leather sleeves that I knew housed his grandmother's prized scores from her days as a concert pianist; and a leather chair worn soft because it was his favorite and he had spent so many hours in it, reading, watching television, or just thinking.

I stroked the chair. How could he have kept something like that from me? Did he have something else to hide, as well?

Then, like a magnet, the piano pulled my eyes across the room, and Abby and her plight jumped back to the forefront of my thoughts. I walked over to the instrument she had played so diligently as a child, and again more recently, and ran the backs of my fingers across the keyboard, producing a layman's scale. What courage it had taken for my sister to sit down before a piano that had brought her applause and slowly, painstakingly, without accurate sound feedback, remaster her skill.

Madame Marek had been no piece of cake. She hadn't taken on just anyone for lessons, and although her encouragement of Abby was always implicit, her actual praise was rare enough that when it came, Abby had known it was well deserved. Whatever it was about Mark's grandmother had fueled my sister's determination.

Pulled by some strange instinct, I opened the lid of the piano bench and riffled through the pieces of sheet music. For the most part, they tended to be Mark's cool jazz numbers, so it was uncanny that I glimpsed the lone classical piece among them: *Tschaikovsky's Concerto No. 1 in B-flat Minor*: "Concerto to the Balloons."

For a split-second, I saw Abby's face at—what was it?— maybe twelve years of age, simply basking in a Madame Marek *"Magnifique!"* It had been Abby's moment of personal triumph, for the composition had been this very one.

My breath came heavily as I lifted it out with slightly shaking fingers. It was just such a part of my little sister, since it had been her all-time favorite. Why, she had even had a poster of Van Cliburn in her room at one time, so enchanted was she by his own moment of glory. He was her golden boy, not some rock star, because he had mastered her beloved "Concerto to the Balloons" and dazzled those at the renowned Tschaikovsky competition.

Gingerly, I opened the sheet music, now yellowed with age. I knew I would never be able to read all the notes, since I had never progressed past Flutophone stage in elementary school, but Abby's eyes had perused these very pages; I desperately needed a connection with her. Certainly in the black and cream of the music, I would find my sister, for music was she.

Like a lone leaf at autumn's end, a loose sheet of paper with no musical notes on it fluttered to the floor. Abby's writing and crossed out words: a draft of some kind it seemed to be. Mark's mantel clock ticked exaggeratedly as I just stared at it, struck by the familiarity of her handwriting.

Then a sentence jumped out at me: *I felt so safe and protected with you.*

"Safe and protected"? Who? With a strange mixture of reluctance and necessity, I picked it up. There was no salutation.

I was suddenly so impatient to read that my eyes, when they finally examined the page, raced so furiously over the words that they could take in only phrases: *starved for connection . . . lifted me out of apathy . . . didn't have to wear my hearing aid . . . listened to me . . . room became a sanctuary . . . .*

And the negative words: *manipulated . . . exploited . . . abused my trust . . . .*

Sickened by what I was reading, feeling as though Abby's words were mincing something vital inside me, I slowed down and read on, and was clued in when I saw: *I found a substitute for my beloved music. Did you put that first book on your desk as a lure, or was it only an accident that you capitalized on later? You knew, didn't you, because you programmed it that way, that I would do anything . . . anything at all . . . not to lose my newfound joy?*

When his name finally appeared near the end of the wrenching draft, I knew without a doubt for whom my sister had intended this letter, and my blood boiled.

More livid than I had ever been in my life, I barged into his waiting room, where a fifty-something receptionist sat behind a half-wall at a desk. As I cleared my throat, she started and looked up from her computer. I was there on a personal matter, I informed her. When I didn't offer more, she reluctantly indicated that he was still in his office.

I took a seat in the empty patient area. A door looked like a gash in one wall, and a taste as acrid as an aspirin melting on my tongue nearly gagged me. What was he doing in his inner sanctum, anyway? Bending another unsuspecting teenager's mind? The quarter-hour, filled as it was by the fresh memory of snippets of Abby's letter that only fueled my revulsion, disgust, and anger as every moment ticked by, seemed to stretch into eternity.

Images of my sister exploded at random and shattered into a mosaic of innocence: the way she had liked me to draw funny faces on her big toes; tea parties; the time we had entertained our parents by presenting a holiday skit; stories of mine that she had drunk in like fine wine; and the dreams and hopes and ambitions she had evinced.

Even after her illness had brought changes that sobered her and cast shadows no one had anticipated, something of the little girl had remained.

All lost; all lost because of this horrid man!

Finally, the door opened and a man in his early forties stepped into the waiting room. Attractive in a gray blazer, he didn't look like a monster, but then, not all monsters did. My hand clenched, unseen, in my lap. Only the thought that he might be a patient kept me from spewing the words that were dammed inside.

When the receptionist walked over to him and their conversation buzzed briefly with a certain familiarity, I knew he must, indeed, be Dr. Richard Damon.

"How may I help you?" he asked, approaching me with a smile. His proximity nauseated me and yet imbued me with a certain restraint.

"I'm Paige Jensen. Could we speak in private?"

He blanched ever so slightly at my name but never quite lost his composure. "You can go now, Marilyn," he called to the receptionist, who had returned to her cubicle.

"Come back to my office," he invited as he began walking from the direction he had come. I hadn't seen a patient emerge, but I remembered that sometimes doctors had second, private doors so that one person didn't encounter another.

I followed, watching his gait, wondering if I made him uneasy. Too angry and sick-at-heart, I was beyond nervousness.

The room was like something out of a film, with an abundance of gleaming wood and green leather upholstery. Even through the miasma of such strong emotions, the things we notice are amazing. Books in cases flanked two entire walls, windows comprised another, and the fourth was plastered with degrees, plaques, and accolades that included photographs of him shaking hands or otherwise being in the presence of dignitaries who included an easily recognizable movie star and an upper-echelon politician.

He motioned for me to sit down in a leather chair opposite his desk. I stood.

"I don't think we have met, Paige, but I heard a lot about you from your sister. I can't express—"

"Oh, cut the niceties! I know all about you, you despicable, degenerate man. You exploited my sister in the worst way, using her naivete and need for human empathy. You saw her sense of isolation, profound frustration, and her resultant apathy, and you gained her trust somehow and then moved in as if she were no more than prey, manipulating her into a relationship she didn't really want and certainly didn't need. Prey, Dr. Damon! Her letter leaves no room for doubt that you not only seduced her but fathered her unborn child. How could you? Didn't you ever look beyond your own depraved needs to think that maybe someone so vulnerable wouldn't be able to handle this? There is no excuse in the world for what you did. You were her psychiatrist, an authority figure, but did you help her, did you even have her best interests in mind? No, you destroyed my sister's innocence. She was only sixteen, and a very young sixteen at that. Only sixteen!"

When I paused to come up for air, he said just one thing. "Let me see the letter."

An alarm blared in my mind at the coldness of his unrepentant response. The letter? Was that all he cared about? It was in my purse, and now I wished I had left it behind at Mark's with the note I had hastily scribbled for him.

Dr. Damon's gray eyes, turned icy, locked onto me, and I said the first thing that came to mind. "It's in my car."

"I'll go down with you to get it."

Cold fingers of uneasiness tickled the nape of my neck. I got up to leave. "I'll mail you a copy," I said as calmly as I could. I had never had such a strong feeling that something was wrong in all my life.

How could I have been so stupid? I had been so caught up in the single-minded task of telling off this poor excuse for a man that it had never occurred to me until now that I might be putting myself in danger by coming here. It suddenly hit me that he would want to destroy any and all proof of his professional and moral lapse. The letter certainly fell into that category.

Any and all proof . . . .

He slid open one of his desk drawers and reached in for something.

Any and all proof . . . . I inhaled sharply. Abby! She and her baby had been proof.

The horrible realization that the man across the desk from me had murdered my sister propelled me toward the door.

I heard the scrape of metal against wood. Then, in a flash, he was behind me.

Caught in a nightmare scene, I was running and not seeming to gain any ground. *Faster!* I commanded my legs, but they couldn't move quickly enough.

His hand clamped my shoulder, and his voice, inches from my ear, whispered, "All you have to do is—"

The sound of sirens wailing in the distance arrested him in mid-sentence. My flicker of relief, hardly born, changed to absolute terror as the hard muzzle of a gun poked into my ribs.

"Come on!" he ordered.

Then everything happened at once. As the sirens screamed ever louder and lights flashed through the wall of windows, the gun moved away from my rib cage, and I made a dash for the hall.

A single gunshot pierced my ears and momentarily rooted me to the spot. I realized he had turned the gun on himself. Still, I ran, ran . . . .

All at once, the hallway came alive with uniformed police officers, and then Mark, whose welcome arms went around me. "Paige, oh, my darling, Paige. Are you all right? If you hadn't left that note . . . . "

As I pressed my face into Mark's strong chest, I murmured that I was okay.

"He's caught," Mark said as he stroked my hair.

Abby had stopped him.

─CHAPTER SIXTEEN─

Nothing would ever make standing at a sixteen-year-old sister's grave right, but as I did so now, with the knowledge that Abby had not taken her own life, a small measure of sorrow lifted.

Although the bullet hadn't ended his life, Dr. Damon would never abuse another teenaged patient. Exposed by Abby's letter and missing journal, as well as by other girls who had come forward, he was through as a doctor; if justice were served, he would spend the rest of his life in prison.

Because she knew that Mark would find it sooner or later, or that she could easily retrieve it if her suspicions turned out to be groundless, Abby had hidden her journal inside one of Madame Marek's leather piano score sleeves. How fortunate it was that Mark had taken several of them with him to Arizona, or heaven only knows what might have happened, for it was my sister's final entry that let him know Abby had very likely been murdered, and by whom:

> *All of a sudden, I'm really uneasy. It was just*
> *something. . . oh . . . cold in his eyes when he said,*
> *"Little girls like you are ripe for suicide or just . . .*
> *vanishing." He likes to test me, to push my buttons,*
> *but was this one more intimidating comment or a*
> *real threat? I have to think about that. All I know is*
> *that if something happens to me, look to*
> *Dr. Damon and this journal for the answers.*

Mark, of course, had been beside himself with worry for me after reading the journal, and sick at heart when he realized that he himself had inadvertently tipped Dr. Damon off. Feeling Abby's secret was too large to keep to himself, yet wanting to honor his promise not to tell our parents, he had gone to no less than Abby's psychiatrist for advice.

My poor sister . . . .

Yet how loved and loving Abby had been! I had always known it, but the copy of her journal given to us by the police only confirmed it most poignantly.

I, as well as my parents, I hoped, now knew Abby as we never had in life—knew her fears, her anger, her struggle, and her triumph. I didn't know where she was now, or even if she was, but I had the conviction that because she had lived, my life and countless others were richer than they would have been without her.

Still, when I saw the name Abigail Lynn Jensen engraved into the red granite of her marker, it seemed impossible that my beautiful little sister, the baby I had held, was gone. I swallowed hard.

Gone. That was the finality of death; that someone could be so . . . gone.

Or was she? Maybe, instead, she had moved from nothing to something to everything, I thought, as a motion caught my eye: a butterfly.

"I haven't seen a monarch butterfly for years," Mark commented from behind, momentarily startling me.

Still watching the grace of the distinctive orange and black form, I didn't turn around. It wasn't that I was still angry at him for not having said anything about Abby's pregnancy. Very simply, he assumed that I had known and found it too hurtful to bring up.

I reached back for his hand as I said. "Neither have I. It's beautiful."

He stepped up until he was even with me. "Butterflies are also symbols of everlasting life."

It brushed Abby's stone and flew upward.

"It's leaving." I said, reluctant to have it go. Maybe Mark heard my voice waver. His arm slid around my shoulders as we stood, still watching the butterfly.

"No, look! It's coming back." His jubilance flowed into me, and as my tears welled and I felt his strength, the butterfly touched my cheek as lightly as a kiss.

Maybe it was only the breeze, but I thought I heard a lispy preschooler say ever so gently, *Paithe.*

Then it soared and was gone.